Green Dust

Preface

Stephen and Lucie went to the same school and happen to meet for the first time since they left.

Stephen knew Lucie well but Lucie had no idea who he was let alone know that he was actually in her class for two whole years.

Their chance meeting was written in the stars but not planned by either of them, but by forces unbeknown to anyone. The situation made use of their scientific backgrounds.

Their journey was to leave them wide eyed and astounded for the rest of their lives. This will remain a secret for the foreseeable future, if there was one…

This novel is dedicated to my wife Andrea for nearly thirty-five years of her Love and unwavering support.
Timmy xxx

Cover inspired by Geralt Altman Pixaby.com

The Mee

It was on July 15th that my Gra
from anything that was spoken
one of many minor illnesses th

Grandma was a strict vegetarian and had been so for many years back to when it was seen as a bit strange. Even so her first words to any stranger or distant family members was about her vegetarianism. She never called it that then but stated "I only eat fruit and vegetables".

This was in case they brought her presents of a carnivorous nature. Her diet played no part in her death as far as we know, we will know more after the post mortem. In fact, that lifestyle choice might be the reason she reached that ripe old age, theories abound for and against the diet, ad nauseum.

Ironic that being a vegetarian was a kind of bonus for her due to weak teeth, the result of a terrible diet during the depression. Most of her teeth were not her own but I guess she had no need for strong chewing teeth just to bite through vegetables and fruit.

Her funeral was anticipated to be in less than two weeks' time, unless the post mortem reveals something sinister, which I very much doubt.

As Grandma had no underlying illness it was deemed necessary to have a post mortem just in case she was murdered in the study with the lead piping by The Plumber. Couldn't resist that one.

I booked myself into a small hotel in town long enough for the funeral and the informal wake and of course an opportunity to meet long lost family members. Some weird, some wonderful like the Munsters in Beverly Hills.

Time also to look around my old school academy in the same town and revive a few memories, mostly good.

I couldn't stay with my parents after they downsized five years ago to a luxury development on the edge of town, an oasis of calm amongst tropical planted palm trees, as described in the brochure. When there were a handful of apartments left and pressure to sell them the description changed and was even more dreamy. Lose yourself in our Garden of Eden, of fruit trees, fragrant roses and Lilly ponds meandering amongst herbaceous borders leading to a communal lake, sheer bliss. The supplementary sales script would offer or send to anyone browsing the website or even walking into the 'dreamy' set.

I drove into the parking lot of the hotel and used the code sent to me for the key safe.

After unpacking the weekend case ready for what could be an intriguing jaunt or a boring visit to my old place of learning.

When I arrived at the school gates, it was not as I remembered at all. It took a while to sink in as to why the school looked so different and far more modern than I had remembered. Perhaps my memory was playing

tricks? After all, a few years had passed. The reason it looked different, I learned later, was that it had been partially rebuilt after a small tremor destroyed one of the school blocks just a couple of years after I left. There on the wall at the side of the school gates was a poster inviting anyone interested, to an opening of the new Observatory by... would you believe my old science teacher Mr. Lintott, now Dr. Lintott the principle. The opening was timed to coincide on what was billed as the best time for a meteor shower, peaking around the nights of 9th and 10th of August that year.

Wow I thought, an observatory, in my old school! It transpired that the building inspector discovered that the science block was built by a different contractor to the rest of the school and from substandard materials and methods not able to withstand minor tremors as specified in the contract, this being California after all.

The subsequent court case was won with ease and with a decent pot of money available for something special the principle gathered the heads of departments, now Deans, in a kind of social get together & brainstorming session taking ideas from the academic group.

The outcome would decide what fabulous technology could be added to this institution that would give them that wow factor, a term often heard in social circles. With a mixture of great ideas one stood head and shoulders above the rest and was suggested by two of the Deans. A state-of-the-art Telescope and Observatory won the vote. Surely the governors would champion this as it would raise the profile of the school academy even more. It could be linked to the studio and computer suite which just happened to be in the far corner of the grounds where there was also enough space to site the observatory.

Then came the biggest WOW in my head. It was a line on the poster.

The guest of honour Professor Lucie Green will be cutting the ribbon.

OMG, I shouted out loud, looking around with embarrassment, checking that no one was near me to hear the outburst.

Fortunately, I had excelled in my career according to the company I work for as a Biologist with a BSc 1st, specialising in Biological Anthropology but Lucie my old classmate of 2000 was now a professor! Not the spotty shrinking violet that I remember, surely not the case anymore?

My interest in Anthropology was ignited when an invitation was received from a nationally respected archaeology unit based in the north of the country to the head of science, who had taken part in several digs as part of his hobby during his student year out. The biology classes were to assist a rather large rescue dig. Sadly, rescue digs are all too frequent these days and happen in the west more often because they are a short quick access to investigate sites of known occupation, often identified by aerial photographs or scans, some back in the 1970s. The term rescue is named as such because someone over time has flagged up a possible dwelling from scorch marks or long shadows in the late evening sun. There may be wooden posts, standing stones, graves or buildings lying beneath.

Today LIDAR is used and gives far more accurate information than an old poor resolution photograph could ever reveal. The land about to be investigated is usually earmarked for building houses or industrial use but not if the rescue dig finds something so significant and historic that it must be preserved. The expense for the dig is born by the developer and should something be revealed and better still intact, the same developer will cough up for plans, protection and revised drawings and worst of all loss of the land.

Rescue digs in London, England found cemeteries containing thousands of Black Death bodies and another right in the heart of the city a perfectly preserved Roman Villa was found with fully intact mosaics. These like others before them must be left in situ and a sympathetic access be created above them changing the proposed building for the future.

Builders & speculators absolutely hate rescue digs mindful that if something is found it wrecks their plans to build, it may cost a small fortune to preserve.

The sifting and screening of spoil heaps in a significant grave site theoretically could prove to be 1500 years or older and rewrite their history should there be signs of earlier occupation than recorded. Burial styles are a great guide with knowledge of the many religions and how they treat their dead. Not forgetting of course that the context in which they are placed in the grave. Were they thrown in a heap or laid east to west or even decapitated. Perhaps some of the bones were deformed or cut. Strangely if the body near a church is not laid like the rest but with their feet pointing towards the church then this might be the grave of the vicar.

A few days after we returned from the school field trip the results were shared with the biology group who were gathered in the main hall.

The bones found at the site were a fantastic record and reflection of the diet and health of those buried and for some, even hinted at their working life.

The teeth when examined for Strontium 90 isotopes gave strong indications that the inhabitants ate a plant-based diet and it showed clear matches for hunter gatherers of north Scandinavian origin. This was the trigger which led to my passion and my career.

Back to the Academy, I decided there and then that I really couldn't miss this opportunity and telephoned the hotel to extend my stay by a couple of days to cover the observatory opening along with a mall shopping trip to smarten myself up.

Even though I had achieved status in my field, I am still in awe of Lucie and just a little nervous about meeting this sweet but homely girl after all this time.

Well, my grandma's funeral was on the 7th which was fortunate that I was able to pay my respects to her, meet the extended family and attend the wake and still make the opening of the observatory.

My strange sister Julia was at the funeral but arrived almost incognito after everyone else. A bit disrespectful I thought. Julia and lofty Husband Marvin Smith were delivered in a blacked-out Ford Expedition that swiftly and deftly vanished as quickly as it arrived. I managed to raise an eyebrow to acknowledge their arrival as they joined the family pews in the chapel. I was unaware then but found out later that they flew into a nearby airfield by military plane and were transferred by a kind of security guy trying to look cool.

This was only the second time, we as a family, had met Marvin. Their first meeting was at their understated smart but quiet wedding. Children were not an option. Lord knows what they do or where they both work, no lifestyle clues were ever given and no one dare ask. We joked that due to Marvins's height perhaps he was a window cleaner without ladders.

Julia used to be quite a sweet and giggly girl but seemed to have had a personality transplant when she married Marvin, the half android.

There were a few third age people from grandma's care home, the only survivors of her generation that knew her.

Grandma Williams had a great life and saw huge changes and events in the world which she would repeat many times even within the same hour. She never referred to her diet apart from the initial meet and jokingly said that the world was slowly catching up to her.

It would be totally inappropriate for me but given her change of diet twenty years ago, I would be fascinated to know the real state of her bones and teeth, much like the school dig results, but, this even in the name of science, I know is a step too far. I kept that thought to myself, just pleased that she had a good innings.

My phone and watch were constantly reminding me that there were things I had to do but it was so annoying it was easy to screen it out for a while. I am also getting multiple emails each asking for a read receipt. Sometimes technology can be a pain.

The text, emails and push notifications are for my up-and-coming trip to India. In fact, it is a trip to India to investigate a group of people practising Jainism, a very old way of life going back over 2000 years. Their diet and beliefs are of real interest to BIOScience Food Corp, my employer.

Their intention is to glean a useful insight into their pure Vegan lifestyle and study the long-term gains and benefits, of how this group of people have adapted to live this way. Almost aligned to fit with my specialism, so not only a huge insight, perhaps material for a future thesis, but massively useful for Bio Science if the results were to lead to better healthy food, but more importantly, cheap food sources readily available and giving healthier margins.

As the day approached and a shopping visit later to the mall to find clothes suitable for a prominent biologist, I felt a little more at ease and as comfortable as it was possible to be, given so many variables.

7.30pm was the official time for the ribbon cutting so I decided to arrive about forty minutes before to look around and familiarise myself with the new build and decide where I should position myself.

As I walked past the school gates I could see a small crowd at the end of the path. My now very old Biology teacher recognised me, surprisingly so and with a huge grin shook my hand and congratulated me on my career path not to mention my entries and articles on Anthropology in the science journals sent to the school. I had completely forgotten about those!

Like Lucie, he too, gained a higher academic level, becoming a doctor.

I was delighted that Dr. Lintott even knew who I was let alone recognise my contribution to my branch of science.

I asked Dr. Lintott where Lucie was and nearly choked when she was pointed out. Open mouthed and flabbergasted would not cover half of the shock that met me. Thankfully I didn't let out another wow, even though it was due. She looked stunning. Dressed to kill "and guess who's dying"?

Lucie was like a red-carpet guest at a Premier, looking like a true Hollywood A-lister. Like most of my school memories a little skewed beyond expectations. She had clearly been to the salon today and spent a small fortune. Well, it wasn't wasted, I can tell you. Her skin was made for high definition. Whether it was naturally smooth or fantastic makeup I do not know. Then there were her cute little dimples, a genetic treat.

My eyes felt like those of a startled cartoon character on long bouncy springs. Then there was the aroma of an expensive perfume clearly worn by Lucie.

Well, this made meeting Lucie even more wobbly legged than I had anticipated. I walked over to Lucie with a huge but nervous grin and said "Hi Lucie", wow you look amazing. No to mention smell divine. I felt like a whack a mole when she said "Hi and you are?" Err, Stephen Williams I muttered, from your class. So sorry she said I think I remember your name, it was a long while ago.

Given my Anthropology background I should have understood the mores of teenage girls which had completely passed me by when I was younger.

Dr. Lintott was watching from the group and could see me crawling into a hole and Lucie glowing at the same time.

He walked over to Lucie and said "aha you have met our eminent biologist Stephen Williams, much like you at the top of his career". It was hard for me not to grin like the proverbial Cheshire cat. "Oh, I don't think so Sir, err, Dr. Lintott", "please! Call me Chris."

Lucie said oops, "sorry Stephen I had no idea. I am delighted to be in such academic company" as she bowed ever so slightly. Dr. Lintott then remarked, "thinking back we had a science journal a couple of years ago that featured you both on different pages. It was pinned on the school board for weeks and made it into the school history book that year."

Lucie looked at me and sheepishly said "so did you come to see me open the observatory?", "No", I said, "my grandmother died". "Oops sorry Stephen, she blushed", "I was only joking". "She is dead but in fact I only drove by here a few days ago and saw the poster and decided to stay on a couple more days to see what it was all about. Now we meet again and I am so pleased I decided to make it to see the glamourous professor."

Her eyes narrowed and I felt like I might have a red laser dot on my forehead. I grinned and showed smiley eyes back. There was a hint of a smile and one of her cheek dimples caught in the light. I melted again.

"How did the funeral go" Lucie said? "I know they tend to be a meeting of relatives not seen for years and some look nothing like you remember." "Like classmates, in a questioning tone?", I added quickly, "it went ok" I said "and a good turnout for our last family member of her generation, thank you".

I quipped, tongue in cheek, "I vaguely remember you from class and was curious to be honest", she got the remark and replied none verbally via her eyebrows in a way that said really?

"Did you get married by the way? I said as casually as I could. "No, I was too busy saving the planet looking out for alien marauders in my spare time", came the reply. I thought really! Is she on medication, looking away in case my face said the same. When I looked back, she was in stiches, shoulders going ten to the dozen and nearly snorting in the process.

"And you" she replied? "Nooo, too busy saving the planet too from potential Alien viruses, much like you". That was a mutual touché.

With that said there was a shout out for Lucie to go over to the entrance of the observatory and prepare to cut the ribbon.

Lucie had to compose herself and fortunately had prepared a few words, expecting that this may be recorded for all time, or God forbid the local media in attendance recording live.

I quick footed it over to the ceremony and with a little pride watched her eloquent speech about being a Class of 2000 student and given the most amazing education here at the Californian Academy of Science and

Technology. Dr. Lintott Praised Lucie for her achievements and the pride felt by the Academy in having Lucie in the pages of Class of 2000 yearbook.

"We are also pleased to tell you that Lucie will be staying on for a few days here as we build a new and exciting programme with our sponsors at JPL and the telemetry and superfast fibre shared between us and NASA. What an adventure this promises to be.

Now feel free to explore the telescope not through the eyepiece but via the screens dotted around as we send our new GOTO scope to one of the 8000 programmed celestial bodies. As the light fades outside you can use the sunbeds placed on the outer wall of this building, curtesy of the Travel and Tourism studio facility".

A few of the visitors approached Lucie to ask questions including a local journalist and a few parents of prospective students excited at the new horizons now available to their bright children. The crowd dispersed and walked around the facility leaving Lucie to come and find me.

It wasn't too difficult, I was following her like a C.C.T.V. joystick controller watching her every move but at a distance, smiling.

She asked me if I had heard the address. "Yes, it was brilliant". She said, "I meant about the sunbeds?" "No, I must have missed that bit". "Follow me" she said and quickly walked outside and around the curved perimeter wall of the observatory where four new white plastic sunbeds with PVC cushions had been placed on the paved walkway. Lucie had taken one of the red L.E.D. torches out with her that astronomers use that allows them to see charts in the dark and then look through the telescope lens without waiting for their eyes to re-adjust.

"We can look out for the meteorites, remember?" Ah yes, I almost forgot. Lucie knew exactly where to look of course as these were called the Perseids because they appeared in the constellation of Perseus. There is a comet that travels around the sun every one hundred and thirty-three years leaving a massive trail of dust and debris in its wake, she said with authority. As we are also travelling around the sun too about this time in August, we go through that pile of dust which is caught by our gravity. Two people like you and me discovered this in 1862 call Swift and Tuttle so the comet bears their name.

We dragged two of the beds together and pushed the other two away just in case other people did hear the address and joined us.

Laying on the sunbeds staring at the five thousand twinkling stars in our field of view was wonderful if a little cold. Lucie being the astronomer, just had to lecture me that in actual fact right now as far as we know there are two hundred billion trillion stars. As we get to peer deeper into space there may be more, who knows? The only twinkling star I know is laid next to me I said. Not a little bit cheesy came the reply as she shone the torch in my direction. Sorry I said I couldn't help it.

After a few minutes our eyes started to adjust to the darkness and we waited for something to show up. Well, it didn't take long. The lower magnitude stars also started to show through, Lucie naming some of the more well-known ones.

For most of the day I was pestered by my mobile buzzing and my linked watch but each time I quickly pressed the button to cancel the notification.

Lucie said "you have been getting a lot of texts for a single person! Ones that you instantly dismiss" "Yes", I said "I am sorry, she is a bit of a pain" I said. "What you have a stalker?" "No, no it's my boss and she is pestering me to finalize seats, luggage etc". "It is a trip I am going on next week for a research project that I agreed to undertake. It is to a Jains village of some 850 inhabitants in a remote part of India near Ranakpur. There I hope to study these people and their vegan lifestyle. They have been genuine Vegans for hundreds of years and my company thought that a study of their health may bring rewards and savings for our marketing and procurement unit looking into raw costs".

"The company to be fair, could gain from the visit and I thought selfishly perhaps, give me enough research data for a thesis, and of course you never know it might also be interesting. Anyway, my flight is in just under a week. I have to say I am really enjoying your company so I have put it to the back of my mind for the time being." "I should be looking forward to this being such a mutually important project but the travelling alone will be two full days. Once I meet my translator Arun, I will know what to expect. I just hope he will have learnt enough to make it worthwhile. Arun told me in an email that depending on the weather preceding the visit it could be quite a scary drive in a Jeep type vehicle to get to this village. There can be many massive pot holes and even flooded river crossings on our intended route."

Lucie said "Hey, this sounds far too important to miss," staring directly into my eyes with sincerity. "Not to mention a bit of an adventure from the sound of it. You can still look forward to coming back here and telling me all about it."

"I expect to spend a few weeks here" she said, "not just a couple of days, once I have permission from my workplace. What we have planned is not a quick fix but quite a sizeable project. My workplace will gain quite a lot from the links I have managed to forge with NASA and the JPL with the help of Dr. Lintott, so I am sure they will give me a bit of time off. My Uni may even want to validate the learning programme and link with the school academy, who knows?"

"I agree, it also sounds an amazing opportunity Lucie and should raise your profile even more."

"And yes", I said, "I will definitely look forward to returning here." I felt excited at the prospect of knowing that Lucie will still be around when I get back, all being well, that is!

What a Shower

Well, one or two faint meteorites passed exactly where Lucie said they would be, followed by a few, nowhere near the anticipated constellation origin.

Their brightness varied quite a bit and as a result so did their colour.

When a particularly bright one flew right across the sky I whispered to Lucie, "you are supposed to make a wish when you see a shooting star," to which she turned partially towards me and said a cynical, "really?"

Then two very bright white streaks lit up the sky both of similar magnitude commanding a quiet wow from us both and a look at each other, non-verbally, did you see that?

 After a few seconds of quiet, I tempted fate in spite of the cynicism by asking asked Lucie "a penny for your thoughts?" Although it was quite dark, she turned to me, lit the red torch giving my face a slight devil looks for sure and said "well, yes", she said, "I was wondering what a spectroscopy analysis of that light would show". "Oh, oh yes that would be interesting," I replied biting my lip as I said it, hoping she didn't catch that in the red torch light.

A few more of the bright shooting stars made an appearance followed by the best shower she had ever seen, me too in my limited celestial knowledge. Lucie got up off the sunbed quickly and took her mobile cut of her handbag walking towards the light of the observatory entrance and texted rather frantically. A reply text came back almost immediately which seemed to calm her down. "Everything alright" I said quizzically, "that looked a bit scary from where I am laying." "No, it's alright" she said "but you know when I said I would like to know what the spectral makeup of those last meteorites streams are? Well, I sent a text to my work colleague Patrick who I know had control of the observatory in Hawaii for three hours tonight and didn't want to miss a thing, in the words of the song. He was already on it, he also sounded perplexed. He too was excited to see such a bright display, hopefully it will make analysis easier."

"Sorry I can't assist you here Lucie" I said. "The nearest I get to visual stuff is bioluminescence."

"I have heard of that" said Lucie, "never seen it though."

"We will know tomorrow she said "but it sure is a surprise to see such a spectacle and it looks to be carrying on as we speak." "Well Stephen" she said in a matter-of-fact way, "you never know one of these days a meteorite spectroscopy may not always show metals and oxides, then you can step in and offer your biological theories."

"Perhaps this is how life on earth started" I said, not a flippant remark as I do happen to know that some Nucleobases have been detected quite recently that are part of the building blocks of life. As we watched even more of the shower only a handful originating from around the constellation of Perseus, with plenty further afield. Lucie went quiet for what seemed ages, obviously in my mind she was analysing what possibly could have caused this shift in activity.

Or was she thinking about me? I hope so.

After another hour we were both feeling a bit worn down and the crowds had all but disappeared. "Is it time to go" Lucie said pointing the red torch at my face again?

"Yes, I suppose so" I said. "I can't see it getting any more exciting." "Cheers" said Lucie as if I meant her exciting company. "No, no Lucie, "I meant the meteors." "You mean meteorites" she corrected me. "YES, them, not you," I said. I offered Lucie my hand to help her up off from the low sunbed at the same time said "let's see if we can grab a coffee somewhere." Unfortunately, as I grabbed her hand, I lost my balance falling on to one of the other sunbeds that weren't occupied. "Err" I muttered as my hand met something on the plastic cover. Using the red torch that Lucie offered me I could see a dusting of what looked like ash from an old barbeque spread liberally over both of the spare beds. Lucie said "I'll grab a sheet of paper from the observatory printer, wait a moment."

Returning with a couple of sheets, one to scrape gently across one of the beds and folding the other to keep the ash particles together. The particles only amounted to a thimble full but enough for me to send to my colleagues.

Lucie mentioned that they have a laboratory at work but geared more to teaching than research so they would have to rely on an agency, "so Stephen, you had better take this one."

I was intending to before she even said it. "I have the perfect colleague in mind" I said.

Now we both have something to look forward to for our return visit. Not sure which is the most exciting I said. It wasn't rhetorical but I didn't get an answer anyway.

Looking at Lucie I said "shall we bid goodnight to Dr. Lintott and head to that all night diner I spotted in town?" "Ok why not" said Lucie "but not for coffee or I will never get to sleep." "I am sure they have Fair Trade coffee" I said. "What?" "Sorry just a silly joke, we can have decaf," "yes good idea." We set off into town observing still more shooting stars as we navigated our way. Then Lucie giggled. "What?" I asked. "I just got that joke about not being able to sleep at night except fair trade." Oh dear! We both giggled. The diner lay up ahead looking empty but for a couple of regulars staring at the wall of bottles. "Well, they won't be sleeping any time soon" said Lucie," regardless of the source." How to ruin a joke I thought.

"Fancy a bite to eat Lucie?" "Not really my kind of place" she said. "When they do salads and vegetarian, they tend to be side dishes and not very good ones at that." "Oh, I didn't realise you were Vegetarian Lucie" I said. "Why would you Stephen we have been engrossed in things astronomical tonight." "Cheese toasty or Panini then?" "Yes, that would be nice thank you."

"What are you having?" "I hope you don't mind" I said "but I would like a steak sandwich." "Of course I don't mind." "Funnily, everywhere I look these days, vegetarian options are popping up. Television adverts and billboards with juicy looking vegan burgers that actually look alright. If I am not mistaken our company is involved in this." "I don't need to eat something that looks like a burger" Lucie said. "I understand", I replied.

Where we sat in the diner the saucer shaped red lamp shades, looked a bit like the ones fitted to dogs after an operation to stop them licking the parts that they would otherwise reach. The light shade directed light down towards the table but cast its light at hair fringe height. The light being quite low illuminated our face and forehead.

I was staring at Lucie's highlighted hair quite intensely until she said "Stephen! You are staring." "Yes, sorry I think you have some bits in your hair that look like the ones on the sun loungers." She pulled my head into the light a bit more, and said, "so have you."

The server came over to our table and asked what we would like. "Two decaf coffees please" with a slight nod from Lucie "and a cheese Panini for my friend and a minute steak sandwich please for me." The server replied "will a cheese toastie be ok as we are out of Pinnies." "Yes, said Lucie that's fine" with a smirk.

The waitress went to deliver the order to the cook. I said "I reckon she is looking up Panini in the dictionary as we speak." "Do you think they will have a dictionary here Stephen?" "Point taken. No."

"What are we going to do about the bits in our hair" said Lucie? "Not quite sure" I replied," I don't really want them in my sandwich." "Do comets carry little bugs?" "Don't be silly." "Do you have a comb in your handbag Lucie?" "I think so, somewhere." "Shall we mount an expedition to find the comb then lol?" "I love sarcasm" said Lucie! "Do you" I said with a grin?" NO!"

"May I also use it, unless it is pink!" "What?" "Do you really think a Professor of Astronomy would have a pink comb?" "Well, you have a pink mobile" I retorted as quick.

"That was a present. Do you want it or not?" "Yes, pretty please, Professor" I said childishly.

We both stepped outside and combed the particles out of our hair. When we stepped back inside the waitress gave us the strangest look, having seen what we were doing very clearly. I said "Oh, we were scraping old paint off the wall and got covered in the dust and debris." The waitress just lifted her head looking at Lucie up and down, as if to say in that dress? "Whatever!", and walked off.

The food arrived as did the decaf coffee and both were devoured with speed but quietly, something mutually appreciated. A coffee top-up came automatically from the transfixed observing server without ordering, fortunately, still decaf. "Well now what," we almost said in unison. "It's been a long day, and a delightful one too" Lucie said, "but my pillow is waiting for me, and me it." "Shall I take you back to your car then Lucie or to your hotel?" "As we walked here, I guess neither of us drive", said Lucie.

"Yes, Lucie I said I do, but I thought the walk was only a short one." "Ok let's do the short walk back to the car at the observatory then back to the hotel please Stephen, I got a cab to the observatory tonight." "Ok no problem" I said, "what are you doing tomorrow?" "I genuinely have no idea" she said "but I am going back to the academy as we announced earlier and I think that might end up being in a couple of days' time. I will be working with the principle to create a plan for the future, and beyond as she stretched out her arm and pointed to the stars in the style of Buzz, lightyear, not Aldrin." I nearly spat the last remnants of my coffee over Lucie but by pure luck I missed.

Her sense of humour was still active even after a long day, I love that.

I took out my work business card which has my mobile number on it and offered it to Lucie.

"If you want to meet up tomorrow," I said with a show of open hands, giving her the option, "no pressure."

The bill was duly delivered to the table, chivalrous without being sexist I casually picked it up.

She was about to say something but I beat her to it. "You can get our next one Lucie" I said at the all you can eat salad bar, with smiley eyes. Lucie got the quip and treated it with the contempt it deserved.

En y va I said as we stood up together. "I didn't know you spoke French" she said. "I don't Lucie just those three words. I remembered them from a French tour guide years ago, waving an umbrella on a trip in New Orleans with my family. I think literally it means one, there is going." "Yes, it does," she confirmed. "I love French, especially spoken with passion".

I then wished I could speak soft gentle sweet nothings in French in her ear, but alas this ability eluded me. I had to make do with pointing at the door and uttering "Infinity" Pursed lips and a gentle head shake were all I got. We walked back to the observatory in only a few minutes whilst watching the continuing spectacle above us and no other words, apart from the overused, wow.

I directed Lucie to my rental and opened the door for her, noticing a dimpled smile in the low-level street lighting. After getting directions from Lucie, I drove to the smart hotel where she was staying. As soon as we stopped, I got out and ran around to get the passenger door but she beat me to it and stood waiting to bid goodnight.

The anticipation was killing me. As Lucie hugged me, I stole a peck on the cheek, exactly as Lucie had expected and predicted, I am sure. She knew I was eager but played it cool as I thought I was. Lucie could read me like a book. A book at this moment in time she wanted to pick up and read a little bit more, *I hope*.

We both smiled as we parted and waved to each other once she reached the lobby entrance. Well, I felt like I was currently on cloud four and a half. More to do I thought to myself. Just don't be too keen and obvious.

I drove back to my hotel, parked up, walked to the room and started to go through a multitude of messages. There were plenty to read as well as the usual trash.

I didn't sleep too well with a myriad of things going on in my head from intrigue and wonder. Both from Lucie and the meteorite shower. Her beauty imprinted firmly on my retina and brain, stopped me sleeping too deep.

In the morning, I had a list of people to ring, the most important I suppose was to inform my colleague David to lookout for my package containing a sealed capsule that I purloined from the science block, thinking that the folded paper too fragile. In the capsule was a tablespoonful of what looked like ash tray flakes.

I had decided that David in the R & D lab was the best recipient for our sample and had the capability of finding out exactly what was contained in the mix. David's often used function was to analyse food stuffs that had either been contaminated by malice or a fault in production. He was jokingly referred to as Poirot for his powers of deduction, but cruel workmates called him Agatha.

If anyone can find anything unusual and spot the obscure it was sleuth David. This sample was not quite the organic branch of chemistry he was used to and some of the tests may require using equipment almost resigned to the junk pile. I know we will not be allowed to buy any new analysis equipment unless we could prove it was for our food processes.

Lucie sent me a text telling me she had messages from Patrick her colleague with Hawaii telescope access. Some of his texts were in CAPITALS. As she read through them Patrick was clearly excited typing them out making several spelling mistakes in the process.

*"Lucie, each of the streaks had the same light signature as each other as you would expect in the case of a single meteorite from the same source. Were they the same source I am now asking myself? I anticipated that you would want more of breakdown based on the anomalies that I spotted, so I ran an ultra-high resolution mass spectrometry. It revealed a diverse composition. Amongst others, **CARBONACEOUS CHRONDRITES** composed of a spectrum of organic molecules also present. As we know, they are linked to nucleic acids which form a part of the building blocks of life.*

We may have proof that these showers and similar were how life and its beginnings were delivered to Earth as croutons in the primordial soup. The THIOL mix was up to 30%!!!

There are other issues, I am sure, but as we are only dealing with the light breakdown it is imperative that we find samples in case any were spotted or found during the shower.

O.M.G. Mind Blown, from Patrick."

Lucie looked at her watch, it was late but Patrick will, she knew, be on tenterhooks waiting for her response, plus she also had other astronomical news for him. Lucie phoned him then relayed their conversation to me.

Patrick this is extraordinary news but I have even better news. I had to tell him to calm down before carrying on. Last night I was with a friend who is luckily a biologist who had an encounter with a pile of ash or dust. He noticed a spread of this dust and flaky particles when he fell and got his hand covered in the stuff. He collected quite a bit from a clean plastic chair, not including his hand contamination though. I helped scoop it up using paper and funnelled it into a small container we scavenged ready to send off. My friend is called Stephen and, in the morning, I will insist he sends the dust and debris to his R & D laboratory investigator where he works. I will see him later and make sure he does send it ASAP. He may have the next piece of the puzzle? Bye Patrick.

Lucie called me early this morning after she found the card in another expedition search of her handbag. It was only 08.30 am so not too early. I was still in bed though, to be honest but didn't let on.

"Stephen! Its Lucie, have you sent the sample off to your lab?" "Hi, err, no not yet" I said, "I thought I would use a courier later today." "No Stephen, send it as quick as you can" she insisted. "My man Patrick, remember Hawaii telescope? well he managed some brilliant high-resolution recordings and subsequent analysis to reveal what looks like life building blocks but said there is more to this." I was already on that page. "Please, please get it sent off." "Oh, My Lucie" I said excitedly "we may have our Swift-Tuttle moment yet! I am on it" I said. Let me get out of bed first I muttered to myself.

"Shall we meet up for lunch after your expedited parcel?" say at the refectory in the academy?" "Yes Lucie" I replied, "12.00 ok?" "Love to" she said. "Bye Lucie must go"... and in my head get out of bed, lazy bones.

I spoke to my workplace to find out which company to use and one that can be trusted with sensitive information. I got the name and address of one that we have an account with and very fortunately they also have an office on the outskirts of town, not too far away. They guaranteed that the packet would arrive three hours later that day. That would be about 1pm at the latest then. It was too early to go to the academy so I drove into town and had a pancake and maple syrup with smoky bacon for breakfast. Proper coffee to wake up ready for whatever science was going to throw at us. It was still a bit early but couldn't wait any longer so I made my way to the academy.

Lucie got there at 12.00, thirty minutes after I arrived and came over to my car. We both went to see the principle and to the share the news and the progress so far. The fact that we were two highlighted pupils from their school, now about to raise a flag in the whole scientific community, with a discovery that may go down in world history, was met with huge excitement by Dr. Lintott.

I informed Dr. Lintott of the sample posting and expected arrival time and indeed where we found it.

He was pleased that the sunbeds played a part in the sampling even if that was not their intended purpose.

Being new and covered, we hope that it helped keep contamination of the dust flakes and ash to a minimum.

Lucie and I collectively explained about the nucleobases that we now recognise, combined with sugars and phosphates make up the genetic code of all life on Earth but I guess we were like telling our grandmother how to suck eggs!

Some of the nucleobases have already been found such as cytosine, uracil and guanine in meteorites that survived the journey through our atmosphere and subsequent impact.

This episode was appropriate for both of us to be equally involved having a celestial origin and with biological content, fortunately we recognised our joint excitement and were careful not to tread on each other's toes, metaphorically speaking.

Dr. Lintott mentioned that he had an email this morning asking if they had by any chance recorded any of the night's activity in any format, from NASA of all people. It appears many of the observatories around the world were frantically gathering data and sharing results. Even SETI were rattled, extra traffic was seen going in the direction of area 51, wherever that is! Roswell was inundated with people driving in and around the town expecting a close encounter too. Conspiracy theories filled social media channels, drowning out reasonable thinking people, as they always do.

Armchair geeks and apocalyptic theorists' rantings made for hilarious reading, almost a comedy script.

I felt a little more pressure now, knowing that my colleague David aka Poirot may either dampen the whole episode with nothing out of the ordinary or raise even more questions than answers.

The three of us sat in the refectory theorising with many what ifs, like the opening scene from War of the Worlds. Little did we know looking back, that this was closer to the truth than we ever dare believe?

It was 2.37pm when David called with a quivering voice that sounded like a ransom captive talking.

I put my phone on loudspeaker so Lucie and Dr. Lintott could hear everything.

"OK, yes", he began, "there were metals like Nickel, Iron and Iridium exactly as you would expect from space, plus a few unidentified elements and compounds not sitting anywhere in our known earthly Periodic table of elements." Deep Breath… "Then there was a biological sequence that looked familiar to me but wasn't, if you know what I mean. I thought I recognised it but nothing matched exactly as I remembered" he said. "Something in the back of my mind was niggling away, possibly sampling from my last job where I worked in the tropical science research lab. I **will** remember, it was a while ago. Leave it with me."

"By the way" he said, "I have sent a small sample to my old lab, in case I don't exactly remember what it was. They may come back with something more tangible."

"Thank you, David, I am so grateful" I said, "and now, I am a little shaken myself, I added. I dare not even say what I am thinking, nor the two people sat with me, they are also shaking their heads. It is too crazy to contemplate right now. Remind the operations director that I am going to India in a few days as planned. Can you send me all this in an email please David." "I can Stephen but the Director has asked that he has sight of it first and said we must record time and date of every document with the company copyright watermarked throughout." "OK I understand" I said through gritted teeth. Commercial interests as always in the driving seat.

"Good Luck David."

Lucie and Chris were astounded and dumbfounded in equal measures.

We all thanked David for his fantastic initial findings and thoughts. Lucie said "Oh my David you certainly have put the cat amongst the pigeons. Now what!", looking at me?

"Well, I am going to focus on my trip" I said, "sadly even with all this excitement going on." David uttered "Bye"

"By the time I get back we should know everything?", shrugging my shoulders and hands in the air "Don't be so sure" said Lucie with Chris just shaking his head and shrugging his shoulders too. "This is how the British Science Museum must have felt before they grabbed their last souvenir procuring the Rosetta stone," I said, with a smirk. "On the precipice of something great guys?" Hmm?

"Lucie, I have passed your details on to David just in case he can't get hold of me in the Indian jungle.

He is also sending you the current findings in a secure document with my birthday as the password". I whispered "13th February 1985". "Almost Valentine" she said, "how sweet" with a beautiful smile. As if my stomach butterflies were not fluttering enough.

"Can you send me the spectroscopy breakdown Lucie please from Patrick, your Hawaii man, and anything you think could help build a picture?"

She looked at me directly almost staring, making me think I was missing something.

I lost myself in her stare for a moment and realised she had makeup on and the same dress she wore for the Observatory opening.

Lucie must have guessed this was my last day and wanted a stunning look, one that I would take with me whilst I was away.

It worked; I asked Lucie "if I could take her photo to keep me focussed" "please do Stephen". Chris was displaying a gentle smile and stood up with us.

My cloud was in the ascendant.

Lucie came closer and gave me a proper hug and a kiss on the cheek and whispered in my ear "I will be waiting". OMG now I am glossing over and the butterflies are taking off.

I resisted the temptation to skip back to the car telling myself I was not five.

I just hope that my jelly legs were not obvious from behind, being conscious that she may be watching me walk away.

I had just over a couple of hours drive to home and checked that my apartment was safe and secure. My checklist was somewhere lying around that I created to make sure I had everything legal and above board.

India

This was an expensive trip so I could not risk wasting money on stupid mistakes.

Passport and visa, company loaded credit card and hundreds of Rupees, like Monopoly money.

I don't take any medication so nothing that could get me into trouble, even prescribed medicine can be against their laws, like codeine.

I had my jabs a few weeks ago thankfully because they hurt like crazy for days. I got a text from Lucie. Did you get home ok? Let me know LX. Short and sweet so I replied the same but with two X's

I leave in the early hours of the morning ready for the long haul of sixteen hours. The paper money is crazy. I have $500 worth but it's over 40,000 rupees. I packed thin cotton khaki clothes in the hope that it is not cold nor constant rain. If it does rain at least, it will be warm rain. The forecast says it is rainy season but I expect it will be sporadic. Food is included on the flights so no need to fill up with any junk food. Alarm set to 1am for a 2.30am departure from home.

Did not sleep too well but then when flying I always seem to sleep light in case, I wake up late and miss the flight. Airport parking was booked for me and easy to find so just security passport and visa checks.

The airport was very quiet and very efficient going through their system. Boarded on time and was met by lots of pretty stewardesses. Spacious seats and I slipping into the arms of Morpheus as soon as I settled down, I was woken in what was morning for breakfast delivery. I didn't recognise all of the food so ate pastries and juice with coffee. Well, that was three quarters of a day I will never get back.

Not sure what the time is here but feel weird anyway. I passed through passport control after multiple questions and collected my suitcase. Looking for Arun or moreover my name Stephen Williams written on a card.

There he was holding up a hand written name that resembled mine so it must be for me.

"Hi I am Stephen Williams, are you Arun?" I asked the young man "Yes, Sir Mr Villiams". "No need to call me sir Arun". "Ok Sir" he said with a head wobble. "We have lots to talk about before we go to village and there is something I must tell you very soon". "I have not been for two weeks and since my visit I am not getting messages. There is no reply to email or phone text from the elders. We must go tomorrow after you sleep". Arun drove me to my reserved hotel getting out to take by bags and simply said "I will be vaiting at the same spot in the morning 9 am" and handed them to the doorman and swiftly trundled off.

I booked in and had a quick look around the lobby. It was very homely and perfumes of various sorts wafted around the wrapped silk pillars. The perfume was not as exquisite as Lucie's though but warm and subtle.

This is the colonial style from The Raj, I believe. Very beautiful.

Up to my large room, my bag was carried at the bell boy's insistence. I gave him a tip but really not sure if it was enough, like an insult or did I give him a month's wage in one go?

First things first, send messages to all that I am safe.

Message back from Lucie *are you OK? Do you feel well? Yes*, I replied *apart from flying in my sleep and waking in another time zone, why?*

Oh, nothing, she put, just checking. Has something happened I quizzed? No, it's nothing, just keep in contact. Oh, by the way David remembered that sequence he thought he recognised. It was not identical to the one they found. Something about a tick bite.

I do know a bit about tick bites and Lyme's disease etc. So, I will be interested to hear what he has to say.

BTW when do you go to the deep jungle? Tomorrow Lucie but it's not like the amazon or anything but it is raining more than I had hoped. Not looking forward to jungle mud! Stephen xx

As promised Arun was outside in a slightly shabby looking Maruti which was covered by canvas but fitted with roll bars. Not sure if that was a good thing or encouragement to take risky dips and hollows.

Off we went into the unknown.

Fortunately, my back was untroubled even after being thrown around a few times in the Jeep type wagon and sent my feet shooting in the air when a filthy mud stream came into the foot well. So pleased I didn't wear white.

Ahead of us I could see what looked like a huge Temple but past that I spied a small hill village near Ranakpur with smaller temple buildings spread out over a couple of miles at a guess. The population was 837 at the last count, according to Arun.

As we drove into what was an old stone built arched gateway into a village square there was no one to be seen. We spotted a man running across and around the back of a building. Running over carefully in the wet gravel he shot out of view. This was very eerie with no sounds to be heard from any direction until it was broken by a metal clanging noise. We both moved towards where we thought it came from and saw a man huddled in a kind of small shelter and a square corned beef can on the floor, obviously the one that made the noise. The man in the shelter, looked to be around thirty, he was rocking back and forth and making unintelligible sounds.

To me they were anyway, but Arun could make out some of his hysterical words. In essence they were "not me" several times and "go away".

Arun tried to ask him questions but he did not react at all as if he was deaf or he was in his own little world.

We left him where he was and looked for more villagers, some that might tell us what had happened. Two people we spotted through an open window, were a couple, we presumed it was also their home. They were huddled together in the bedroom and so still as to look like they were in suspended animation but they were alive, just like the other guy we saw, but making no noise except for a very low whimper, almost an internal cry. We looked around for clues not knowing what we were actually expecting to see. This without doubt was the strangest of situations I have ever been in. I checked that water was available in the various outlets dotted around the village. At least the solar powered pumps were keeping them going. Although the villagers here do not welcome visitors, according to Arun, certainly not tourists, they do accept help with the functionality of daily needs.

The food larder in the house we checked had a few items in baskets and oddly another couple of cans of Brazilian corned beef that was concealed wrapped in a blanket. Only when I remembered the purpose of our visit did it occur to me that there should be no meat here at all. Beef in India is decreed as sacred in eighty percent of the population so this is a double no-no for this small devout Jains village.

After what seemed like hours we discovered more people in a state of shock.

One man started screaming the second he saw me. He looked directly at me and shouted "Devil" with horrendous fear in his voice. Arun had been crying from the tear marks on his cheeks that I hadn't noticed at first being so focussed on our victims.

I am not sure if it was the horror of the situation for his fellow countrymen or the moral transgression of beef eating against their religion and belief. We used our phones to take photographs of the desolate place trying not to snap the handful of victims we found so far.

I suggested to Arun that we take one of the cans of corned beef just as a precaution in case the contents had poisoned everyone. That would not account however for hundreds of missing people nor bodies. There were no signs of any struggle or gunfire. No burning found either. Could they have thrown themselves over the village walls in some kind of cult following suicide? We tried a few more houses as they were dotted around the hillside but only found about twelve people in total. We saw more empty corned beef cans strewn over the side of a small ravine, like a calling card of a serial killer leaving one heck of a puzzle.

Not wishing to stay here waiting for the night to descend and we suffer the same fate as these poor people we knew we had to leave to get a message to the outside world. Neither of our mobiles had signals and we saw no power being used by any lights or equipment. Fridges were not working but the produce was not stinking or mouldy so we assumed it had only recently stopped.

The authorities were hours away but a few miles before we got to the village, we passed a small hamlet that had a filling station and a tiny café. With any luck there will be a phone we can use to raise the alarm. This is like a horror film with way more questions than answers. Lucie will never believe this Mary Celeste scenario, nor will anyone else without any proof or hard evidence.

We realised that there was little we could do here and should leave the authorities to work out what had taken place. We should also leave as soon as we could.

We left in a sad melancholic mood knowing that there wasn't going to be a great outcome to this; how could there be?

We still had good light for the treacherously poor roads and monsoon flooding which had been kind to us. It took nearly two hours to get to the hamlet and the café was still open but the filling station was closed. The café did have a payphone that only took coins of which I had none, however the café was more than willing to help once Arun told them of our findings. Krishna the café owner was visibly upset during the conversation, understandably so when he told us he has a cousin there. Arun managed to speak with a policeman in a provincial station and left our details with him. He found it hard to believe what we were telling him asking if this was a hoax or a prank but no sadly it wasn't. Arun told the officer that we will be travelling into Jaipur and will both make a full statement there in the morning.

This appeared to be acceptable from what I could make out. We had a snack and drink and left for Jaipur

We arrived back at my hotel around 6pm just before sunset.

Arun said we should go to the police station in the morning because if we go now, we will not get to sleep tonight. Why I said, they are not being very quick was the reply, much paperwork.

A long hot shower was so welcome along wi a proper coffee.

There was a selection of snacks in my room which was all I could manage. The Bombay mix was very spicy; a lot more so than I have had before. I fell asleep half way through eating some interesting biscuits, very odd selection though.

The morning call and text pings did not allow me to sleep in.

Arun was due at 9.30 so I had just enough time to grab a continental breakfast, or so I thought. It was 8.15, I made the mistake of looking at my mobile as I took the lift to one of the dining rooms. Being out of touch yesterday was possibly the best, considering the quantity of emails, text and messages that I had.

I could see Lucie, David, my food company, work director, government info. OMG what the heck is going on? From Lucie, *are you well, is everything OK. There are hospital admissions from what we don't know.*

There have been bulletins asking people to be vigilant but unfortunately, they haven't said about what!

From David;; *I have, with the help of my old colleagues managed to recognise some of the bio-signatures from the dust you sent me with slight variations, which I don't get! This is a new twist based on a recognisable bite from a Lone Star Tick. This has been given the acronym STARI2. Southern tick associated rash illness V2. Although this is not just from the south but the country or even worldwide. We don't yet understand the context of this. If you have any thoughts Stephen let me know what they are.*

The lobby rang my room to say that my guide Arun was waiting for me in the lobby but I missed it being in the lift.

I made it to the dining room but then I was grabbed by staff due to the emerging situation, whatever that was!

The head of the concierge walked me towards Arun, croissant in hand giving me milliseconds to take my first bite when the taxi driver spotted me eating this gorgeous flaky and messy pastry at the same time Arun was saying "good morning" with a head tilt.

The Taxi drive shouted "NO FOOD"! Looking at the pastry half in my mouth, forcing me to drop it in the gutter and it being consequently picked up by the same concierge in disgust.

Having licked the remnants of the pastry off my lips I said "hello, morning Arun," he just stood shaking his head and then held his hands up in a, what the heck is going on type way.

"We must be not telling them about the mad people we have seen in too much detail or we will be living in the police station." "Ok" I said, not really knowing how they could stretch this out to be honest.

The drive was not very far, partly because we were in the centre of the city anyway. Arun had the name of the officer he spoke to yesterday so he asked to speak to him and gave his name. In less than a minute there were seven people surrounding us, only two in uniform. One of them had an earpiece and was talking as he walked up to meet us. He introduced himself to us as Peter. Really, I thought to myself. He looked nothing like a Peter until I recognised a name that sounded like Interpol bureau in amongst the conversation. I could hardly make out what was going on due to the language barrier so I was relying on Arun to make a statement and get us out of here. There was a young lady transcribing as they spoke but mostly no one spoke to me. Several people were asking questions at the same time all focussed on rattled Arun. I could see he was not just irritated at the way they were attacking him from all sides but clearly worried as well. He managed a glance over to me as if to say help me here but what could I do, I can't even speak the language.

Then one of the men turned to me and in beautiful posh English accent, said "how are you involved in this? "

I told the truth of course that this was a trip to study a village that practices Janism in isolation. The company I work for wants to understand their culture and eating habits.

We had no idea anything like this was going to happen. Arun told me that he had not heard from his contact for two weeks so we must go and visit them as soon as possible without delay. When we got there the place was deserted but for about twelve people who appeared very frightened. "Of what" he asked? "I have no idea" I said "and the few words spoken to Arun did not help".

"Have you been to India before?" "No", I said. "Do you have any relatives living here?" "No" again. "Who did you tell that you were coming here? It wasn't a secret so almost everyone I know to be fair. My parents and sister, my colleagues at Food Sciences, my friend Lucie and her University. Two laboratories back in the States". "Why did you tell all these people?"

"Well, it was a very important study trip and the other people had knowledge of the sampling from the meteorite shower that we gathered just before I left". "Where is this sample", he said eagerly?

"I sent it to my company's laboratory, all of it".

"Why is this so important" I said with a slight tremor?

He didn't get to say another word when a suited gentleman entered into this now very crowded room, every one of the seven people stood up. He looked at me and said "Stephen"? "Yes", I replied. He handed me a basic mobile and uttered, "agent Smith for you".

I must have looked pretty vacant at this point not to mention a little worn down. "Yes", I said nonchalantly. "It's Julia" she said. "Who"? "Julia your sister", "stop messing about". "Why the hell are you ringing me, AGENT! What?"

"Look, no time to explain. There is a car outside waiting to take you to the airport right now". "But I haven't even packed back at the hotel I said". "No, we have". "Now leave this interview and get in the car, we have your papers.

What about Arun? He will be looked after, do not concern yourself, he will be fine". "What's all this WE?"

"STEPHEN! Just do as I ask". You could blow me down with a feather. I feel like I am in the middle of an international incident, and it's all my fault. Or have I been fed some bad drugs?

The car was no ordinary vehicle; it made me laugh when I saw the blacked-out windows embassy plates and the feel and sound of a gentle but powerful Bentley.

There was a smoked glass barrier between me and the driver, not, I hope, one that allows gas in the compartment of the occupant! Mind wandering. Too many spy novels, I guess.

We arrived at the familiar airport but carried on through a gate and barrier which lifted as if by magic so we could cross the perimeter over to a waiting grey aircraft. Not the usual colourful plane I catch to go on my holidays. This was much smaller. My first thoughts were, this is far too small to get to the US in one go. Climbing aboard with two men in black, one carrying my suitcase and the other with a briefcase, one in front one behind as if to stop me running away. Walking through the hatch was like a Willy Wonka factory moment and the biggest eye opener of my life. I was asked to sit on a particular seat.

I have never been in a five- or six-star hotel but if one could be fitted inside a plane this would be it. I wish Lucie could see this. I took out my mobile to take a photo and was stopped immediately by one of the men. "If you take any photographs, we will destroy your mobile" he said. "In fact, please hand your mobile to me for safe keeping. It will be returned to you when we disembark".

"So, no chance of duty free then I added" flippantly. That was met with a poker face. Another crew member offered me food and drink from a large tray, no alcohol, which was not five stars but adequate. It was chicken or lamb curry. I opted for the lamb. Beautiful curry, in fact the best I have ever had, although it was a little hotter than I am used to. I managed to eat half of the curry and left the rest.

I saw no uniforms at all from any of the crew until the cockpit door opened and I recognised a smart military style jacket with gold stripes adorning the collar, sleeves and shoulders. The plane looked to have about twenty superb seats in sumptuous cream leather. There were no screens to watch but I could see an obvious large contraption mounted near the front. The odd thing which I didn't notice at first is that there were wires and beautiful copper type pipes almost like a steam punk exhibit. It looked really fantastic and so awesome like the last use was for a ComiCon set. Then a message played over the intercom. Indian regulations require us to vaporise an insecticide inside and outside the aircraft before take-off. Please do not be alarmed. I could see the mist and hear what sounded like a mini gas leak, then nothing. We took off so smoothly and quiet that I thought perhaps the mist was a travel suppressant like a sea sick pill, not insecticide. I asked one of the men what speeds will this plane fly at? He said faster than you think sir. I heard a noise behind me and turned around to look but was unable to focus on the back of the aircraft. I put this down to my awful ability to suffer vertigo at the drop of a hat. I am not very good at fairground rides and become dizzy and sick very quickly. This is how I was feeling right now only worse. My periphery vision was becoming blurred adding to the nausea. Being so tired and as if to prove my theory I fell asleep. I am sure I fell asleep if only to take the sick and dizzy feeling away.

That is the last I can remember.

I felt incredibly poorly and had a memory of throwing up, but not into what or where or even when I don't know.

Something touched my cheek but I had no power to pull away only just enough energy to turn my head to see what was being stuck to me.

I witnessed a misty blurred vision at the side of me that slowly focussed into an alien in my brain but it was Lucie in a grey lab suit. Alien turned Angel. I very gradually got my bearings, lying in a bed still unaware of what had happened. Next to Lucie was Julia my sister and two other people at my bedside!

Julia was looking way smarter than she did at the funeral. Once I was able to focus fully, she shocked me how smart she was. Lucie was my alien, angel. One of the other people was David from work, the greatest surprise of all. It was then that I questioned who had brought all these people together. It was the man in black. His name was Agent Green, no relation to Lucie.

We need to give you a little more time to recover he said then we will all start to try and piece together what we know thus far.

"Very lucky for you Stephen" said Julia "you were sick on the plane after your meal". "Once we spoke to David and just happened to mention that you fell ill on the plane the first thing, he asked was what Stephen had eaten. Fortunately for you, David here, immediately realized you were displaying the symptoms of STARI2, the lone star tick infection when it was confirmed that you had a lamb curry on-board. The puzzling thing is you were not bitten by any tick beetle due to living hundreds of miles from the states known to have the insect.

David assumed that you must have ingested this either through the air or from your hand gathering of the dust which we know contained the odd bio signature.

David as we now know recognised a similar pattern in the SARI bio make up, so we knew how to treat you. Not that there is any cure if it turns out to be true.

Lucie came close again to me and said quietly with tears in her eyes, "I was really worried Stephen after Julia contacted me. I can't begin to imagine how you feel after your trip went so badly".

"This is one huge nightmare I said from touchdown in India". Agent Green stepped in and said this is why we brought you all together, he looked at Agent Smith, Julia. "Yes", said Julia, "we have organised this conference meet. You are inside one of our hubs".

"Where is here", I said? "I can't tell you Stephen", Julia replied. "Your friends and colleagues were all transported here incognito, so they don't know either".

"We have some theories about the last few days but between us all we were hoping we can fit the pieces together. We have people around the world facing the same quandary so someone somewhere will figure this out and we can then counter what is happening.

After David identified that bio bug, we passed this on to our agents around the western world who in turn notified hospitals what they should be looking for, because as you can probably imagine there are many admissions, with very few people in the know. There are over 200,000 patients as we speak being treated for similar symptoms to yours Stephen, only they have no idea where this came from. We think you have a good idea especially with sleuth David here on the case", she looked over to a perplexed David. David and Lucie, "have they intercepted everything we sent to each other" I said? "It looks like it," said Lucie.

Agent Green grinned, he told us that they would leave us to get some rest and will try again a little later if you feel up to it. In the meantime, feel free to relax in the adjoining rooms David and Lucie".

We looked at each other, rolling eyes and shrugging shoulders. "Any idea anyone"? Said Lucie.

David perked up; "well, given a short plane ride it could be any air base within five hundred miles from home. What about Area 51" he said.

"No, it can't be" I said "it doesn't exist". "Only on maps" Lucie interrupted. "That's under five hundred miles" I said.

"Are any of those agents' aliens," said David. "Hey you are talking about my sister" I said. "Then again, ha-ha".

"Anyway, I said what am I going to eat from now"? "Vegetarian" quipped Lucie with a smirk. "Have you caused this Lucie just so we can eat together?" "Yeh right", she said with smiley eyes.

The ceiling of the room we were in, had an attractive colour banded light that we saw illuminate in different combinations. The bands looked like a giant fruit Polo stuck to the ceiling. I guess they set the level of danger or status. They might simply be a messaging system for all of the agents here, who knows.

Lucie added, "guys, they will be listening in to this so just me mindful of what you say. I am sure they will, because it is a secret bunker or something". "Sorry" David said, "I didn't mean it Julia", looking up at the cameras on the ceiling. "*I* never thought you were an alien"!

Lucie snorted, I gave her that look which made her snort again, louder, making it worse.

"If the research is to be believed David you stated that I should be ok with chicken and fish. Ah but then you said that this is STARI2 and not the same as STARI so *will* I be safe"?

"I have no idea" he said "and being locked out of my lab right now I can't even look into it".

Lucie asked me if I felt like getting up and out of the bed.

True I was groggy but able to stand on my own two feet once again, "yes, I think so". "Are you decent" she said? "Always" I replied. "Oh", she said with a hint of disappointment or did I just mishear?

My gown was not an operation one so it was not open at the back. We sat facing each other on soft comfortable chairs and began to question everything we thought we knew.

"David, you kicked this off with your analysis of the dust". "Where do you want to start"? "Well credit where credit is due Stephen and Lucie, if you hadn't sent me the dust, we would have nothing to go on". Then Lucie looked to me "if you weren't the gentleman that you are, you wouldn't have slipped offering your hand to help me up". "C'mon let's stop the what ifs and concentrate on the story so far".

"David, you have the floor".

OK so we have a meteorite shower that was bigger and brighter than most of those that have gone before. Agreed Lucie? "Yes, in living memory". The composition of the ash was also pretty much the same as we expected with the exception of a biological twist. Yes, she nodded and so did I. Apart from the bio bits were there any compounds, elements etc. identical to those we usually see?

NO, well a couple said David but there were some elements or compounds that did not sit within our Earthy periodic table.

We did find Boron which although not very rare on earth, it is present on Mars and also in the sample you sent us. Titanium Sulphide which does not occur on earth but is also in the sample. There is something which sits between the elements of Tungsten and Rhenium at a specific atomic weight of 185.618. We have nothing in our table that matches this. It might be a metal sitting between two metals. Both by the way have very high melting points, useful in the space industry. Rhenium is used in turbine blades but it is also extremely rare on earth. Just suppose there are little green men involved, or women Lucie quipped with smiley eyes, flying saucers made from this metal?

"I suppose they could be women" said David after all some are believed to have crashed. "OI!" Blurted Lucie. My turn for a snort whilst looking at Lucie who was shaking her head but grinning.

The next thing we need to do is replicate the Bio signature and check that the Alpha-Gal Syndrome is identical to the original from the Lone Star as opposed to the dust. We may need some blood from you Stephen to check against blood of a type 1 infection. Sadly, we will need to use an animal to confirm the reaction.

Also test with other meats Stephen, so for the moment stay away from all meats until we know. "You will survive" said Lucie, "join the gang". "There is always fake meat Stephen, some is so good I am told it is hard to tell the difference". "Yes Lucie, so I am led to believe from my work colleagues I said, and the TV adverts of course, always truthful".

"Would you believe me if I said Bio Food have invested millions in alternative meats and have several working meat free partners? I was part of the research project Lucie", added David. "I didn't know that David" I said. "I think it was before you joined the company, Stephen".

"Our company sent me out to these factories when production was under way. Never met so many odd people in my life. Some were caricatures and just hilarious to watch in action, like a slapstick buffoonery type theatre without the intention of being that way. Fascinating to watch and very entertaining nevertheless".

"Sadly, the scenes we met in India are still under investigation" I said, "not by us I hasten to add. Unfortunately, we gleaned nothing from their way of life, food sources nor any health benefits that may have resulted from it. Just a huge mystery that will unfold with time, I guess. Whether we will be a part of that remains to be seen.

An agent came into the windowless suite and said "well that was excellent people. Can we move to another operations room where more will become apparent as the situation unfolds"

The red and green band lit on the fruit polo.

"Stephen, are you ok to walk with us?" "Yes, I am ok thanking you. Some proper clothes would be good though". An agent appeared in minutes with a bag containing trousers and shirt both in my size. We followed the agent through doors after I changed in the men's room and walked down corridors with no markings on the few doors we passed except for single letters or symbols, some were Greek, others no clue.

The doorway we walked through was like NASA mission control. Screens and operatives everywhere. Up above there was another fruit polo this time the red and green were flashing.

A large world map projected up on the wall at first glance was a normal projection until someone walked behind it then it was clear that this was a 3D laser projected scan type screen. The overall sound was fairly quiet like a non-pushy marketing call centre.

I couldn't make out what they were all looking at on their individual monitors or what they were saying due to their headsets and close mics, but the world map gave a clue that this was not just the USA.

Agent Green opened a room adjoining the control room but with a window facing the world screen.

It was hard to work out the context of what we were seeing with flashing red beacons and multi-coloured lines. We could however see the BREAKING NEWS scrolling along the bottom of the projection.

Then seeing, INDIA *code 59* (838) A4f, got us all thinking.

Staring at each other as if to say what do you make of that? Then agent Green broke the non-verbal language going on with… "So let us share with you what we are able to, and perhaps you may see things a little clearer with a greater part of the picture. What you see here is obviously a world map with lots of markers, connected lines, figures in various colours and bracketed numbers. As you can see from the breaking news, we have added the findings from Stephen and Arun and shared this with our operatives around the globe. Code 59 refers to missing persons in the context of the last two weeks. The bracket represents the number of people missing from that area and if the number is red then those figures are confirmed. If in orange then they have been reported as unaccounted for without verification as yet.

This may or may not be connected with the hospital admissions we now have across our country and from correspondence with many other countries. Those currently in hospital relating to this are in violet.

The lines you see are extrapolated directions of the meteorite streams in the hope we can find a point of origin. The white dots are the thousands of objects in orbit around our planet, whether geo-stationary or moving like the ISS for example". Lucie whispered Space Station in my ear. As if I needed telling. "So, 838 if I am reading this right is the actual confirmed missing from our village. What is the A4f then" I said. "Sorry, that is classified Stephen. You will see also violet numbers dotted all over the globe and if you stare at any one set you may see the count going up. Any white bracketed numbers are deaths from those hospitals and the violet figures decremented to show this too".

"On the right margin there are several amalgamated stats by continent, country and cities".

Lucie spoke for the first time in ages as if her scientific brain was trying to compute the myriads of things going on and what their context might be. "And those lines?"

"I can tell from the lines that several converge from hub orbits or is this just line of sight?" I jumped in before agent Green could say anything". "Yes, Lucie looking and counting, there does seem to be a spread between the handful of hubs and similar numbers to each stream as if the workload of the satellites had been shared". "Well, spotted you two", Agent Green said. Then Lucie carried on, "so have you got the stats from the geo-stationary military satellites that we use for our Satnavs, because they are much further out and may give more accurate directional status from those hubs?" "Do these same satellites also provide survey ground references Agent Green? And also, do they record omnidirectional data which would be invaluable if they do". "Well Lucie you really have given this your all. Sorry Lucie, some of that is currently classified but I can tell you that our people are on the same page as we speak, great minds think alike as they say".

"What you have suggested is extremely relevant so I will pass all that you have said to our people and see if it helps to find the origin beyond those hub orbits as you described them. I have to tread carefully here as I am sure you understand we have people with a similar skill set to yours and don't want to make them feel redundant".

Now it was my turn to ask a question with a great deal of self-interest I asked, "looking at all of the hospital admissions around the world that we know about, are any of those hospitalised people, Pescatarian or Chicken only consumers? Sorry just trying to perceive if this bug is wide ranging or targeted". "No", agent replied.

David kind of replied, "great question Stephen", then added, "well the original tick bite gave rise to Alpha-Gal Syndrome. What have you called this one by the way, as he looked at Agent green?"

The agent said "I am not aware of a name or mnemonic yet but we will let you know when one is given".

"We do need to take a blood sample from a sufferer to compare what components are resident in their body and how they vary from the original", said David. "Stephen?", looking towards me. "Yes, I knew I might be your guinea pig David, given that I am the only one you know with this new strain". "Is that a yes then?" "Why not" I said. "If half of the world have no idea what they are suffering from, the least I can do is offer an insight?"

I repeated my question regarding Pescatarian and chicken only diets. This is a question worth asking from the hospital returns data. "We will pose the question Stephen to some of the hospitals but I doubt that this is foremost in their minds right now however useful it may be to you".

David clearly wanted to cheer me up by mentioning Pork-Cat Syndrome which was discovered when Alpha Gal was being researched a few years ago. "But I don't often eat pork" I said "and certainly don't eat cats". "Urgh" said Lucie, "disgusting". "No, it is not eating cats Lucie & Stephen but an allergy to cats from their liver crossed with pork albumin. It too can be fatal". Lucie looked at me shrugging shoulders as if to say, oh dear what a shame, never mind Stephen. "Any more delightful consequences" I asked?

"No that's it for now but a lot more research is required".

All through this discussion we could see the control operatives turning to glance our way occasionally.

"The six-million-dollar question ladies and gentlemen is WHY?" As we gather more data it may become clearer.

"Is this a fluke of a contaminated meteorite that became detached from another heavenly body and splattered Earth with its detritus? A bit like the seeds of life David & Stephen, crashing to Earth adding to the primordial soup?

Then again is it an attack on our planet to give another species a home?"

Lucie chipped in "heck that is a huge leap, Agent Green! Unless you know something, we don't?""

"That would be classified" we almost said in unison.

"Well, I have to tell you that your collective insight has been miraculous". The moment he said that the whole of the control room turned to face us and quietly applauded. Well, they were sat the other side of soundproof glass!

"OMG they were all listening in" I said, "Yes" Agent Green said "and acted immediately on what you were postulating. Your contribution has been immeasurable and will most definitely be recorded in science journals in the near future, I am sure".

"Thank you for your cooperation and in order for us to keep in touch there are three mobiles assigned to each of you. They will work anywhere in the world but only between each other and myself Agent Green and Agent Smith. They are not connected to any social media or the internet and their number is completely hidden. 1 is Lucie, 2 is Stephen and 3 is David. No other numbers can be dialled.

I am #, Agent Smith is * Simply press and hold one of those to call, or press it twice to send a text. I may ask you for updates but as you have already gathered, we are aware of your communications and whereabouts.

Please do not divulge any of this to anyone outside of our group of four. We will ask you all to sign a non-disclosure agreements and failure to follow this, may have severe consequences, punishable in law.

You may drop out of this right now but you must sign this agreement in order to be released and never talk of this again. Any questions?" David then asked, "what about our regular work for Stephen and I?" "You and Stephen are under our guidance and have full clearance from your company with their thanks and blessing". "They have also been informed by the White house that your contribution in this matter is of National Importance and have listed your company as an Honourable establishment for the USA. A huge commendation that will open doors for them as an organisation. The same goes for you Lucie. The university have received a citation from the White house for your patriotism towards your fellow Americans. For your contributions and ongoing patriotism, it has been agreed to give each of you a citizen medal. These are not given out like candy but we may be facing an uncertain future and we thought we ought to recognise your work and powers of deduction already. Your certificate will simply say awarded for exemplary work in your field".

Agent Smith, Julia, then entered the room holding a folder containing papers for us to sign to accept the citations and medals. Plus of course the certificate and the small lapel medal. She hugged me for the first time in twenty years as she handed me the papers and badge.

She also said in a soft voice, "well done Stephen we are very proud".

Julia handed the others their paperwork and badges and shook their hands at the same time saying "well done".

The mobiles were handed over by Agent Green with a verbal reminder of our own numbers. "Should you lose or have the mobile stolen contact your friends as you would normally only asking them to contact me, nothing more. *That is important.* We are not the only people that can intercept your messages, emails and voice calls!"

"Ok people we will take you back the way you came, in secrecy of course, follow me".

I asked to go back to the Academy as did Lucie, not least because we had a lot to discuss. "David where do you want to go?" "Back to my lab if I can with some of your blood" he said. "OK Dracula". I looked at Julia expecting her to pick up on this. "Yes, ok Stephen we have a medical facility here but I will ask one of the nurses to come here. Is that, OK?" "Yes, no problem, Julia". David asked if the sample will be given to him to take back. "No" replied Agent Smith, "it will be sent to your lab for your attention and in very safe keeping. It will get there before you".

Well, the stunning nurse came in and my tongue fell out. Lucie gave me the filthiest look, oops. Not content with just one tube of blood but she took three. I asked for a drink and cookies but again got a look, this time from Julia.

Band aid fitted and then Julia said "bye" to us all and a wink to me. Very out of character indeed. "We may see you sooner than you think if our intel is to be believed".

Goods were gathered and we were ushered out through doors and down corridors until we were in a garage lot underground. It was very warm outside but only for a few seconds as we stepped into the blacked-out SUV with the air con set to deep freeze, I think.

We were in the SUV only for thirty minutes looking out nearing twilight. With a handful of stops and turns but a pace that would earn a speeding ticket for sure. We clearly had unimpeded passage wherever we were going. A small airport it seems with two small jets waiting. Two jets because David was going back to work and Lucie and I were going to the academy.

When I say airport, it was over exaggerated. There were no buildings just pale runways and a wind sock hastily erected, I guess.

Distant buildings had lights on but none bright enough to discern anything, so no clue where we were.

 We were met as our vehicle door opened, by two black suited men, very close to the ordered private jets both grey without any discernible markings. They may have some but the dusk light made it difficult to see.

They must still have a designated I.D. so maybe they covered them until we boarded.

Lucie and I were directed to one jet with a six-step stairway and directed David to the other one a few yards away.

On-board the private jet it was smart and comfortable but not lavish. There were only about ten porthole windows, which turned into none at all, once Lucie and I were inside the plane, until take off then it appeared.

How did they do that? Were they painted on the outside?

Well, where we sat there was a window but when I looked closely it was an oval monitor screen. It was dark so could not see much. There must be a tiny camera on the outside that allows the screen to display the same view as a window would.

We had the jet to ourselves but for the suited cabin attendant which if he heard me say that might correct me to, operative? Is this a CIA operation I asked eliciting a glare from Lucie? **No,** he said. Stephen this is a big boy's game now. OK. I get it. Humour I suppose is my cover for nervousness. I have to say this is getting quite heavy I said and I am trying hard to play it cool.

Lucie changed the subject deflecting more silly remarks from Mr Cool. "Where are we going to stay when we get back to the Academy Stephen?"

"Sorry I haven't given any thought to that." The operative came over to us with a tray of drinks and a selection of sandwiches mainly cheese and tomato, salad sandwich, egg mayonnaise and a humus pot with bread sticks. "Wow", sarcastically spoken, "welcome to my new world I said, thank you". I chose cheese and tomato and a cola. Lucie said "great selection, thank you" and picked the egg sandwich and the humus pot. She asked for just plain water, which was on the tray and pointed out by the server. My grandmother would be very pleased to see me eating her kind of food, I think.

"By the way we have taken the liberty of setting up a safe house not too far from the Academy"." Are we in danger we said together, looking at each other as we said it?" "No not as such but we do need to keep things low key until we know more about the whole situation". "Thank you", Lucie, replied. Well, that did not help at all I said to her, feeling unnerved. Just be sensible Stephen we are in very capable hands, to be sure.

I could sense the drop in height after another forty minutes and like magic, porthole windows appeared but only where we were sat.

This is really science fiction I said to Lucie I have never seen anything like it, OMG.

She seemed blasé about the magic windows.

"We are stepping into a world we know nothing about Stephen.

I am sure what we are embarking upon could be mind blowing and reading sci-fi fantasy novels is not helping any of us at all". "I am not into fantasy" I said. "Really, could have fooled me".

Our First House

We landed and as soon as the engine stopped the windows disappeared as if they were never there.

We could see that this was a normal airport but we were a couple of miles away from the terminal buildings. Out of the plane and into another partially blacked out car. Not that this made much difference because it was dark so all we could see were lights on the runway and white lit buildings, no signs.

We were back at the Academy in just over an hour and drove past it by a few hundred yards when we were asked to get out and follow the front passenger who was there all the time without our knowledge.

He was not dressed in black but scruffy jeans and a T-shirt. I suppose he just wanted to look normal.

Our travel bags were handed to us to carry ourselves. The T-shirt guy walked up to a detached modern house in the outskirts of town and used a key to open the front door. We were right behind him as if being shown a new house rental.

Lucie immediately went upstairs and chose her en-suite bedroom. My room would I guess be the next biggest.

There was traffic movement outside yet the house was totally silent, eerily so.

It was furnished, but not by a family from the cold feel of everything. I guess this was a brochure order online and reminded me of a walk around IKEA. Smart, neat and functional but not lived in. The kitchen looks to have everything, but in pristine condition. "Lucie, do you think this place has been lived in? The oven is spotless, there are no food marks anywhere, not even inside the microwave. The refrigerator is also unused". "No, we might be the first" she said, "either that or an ocd cleaner lived here".

"Lucie, without being too personal, I suggest you undress in the bathroom after hanging a towel over the mirror, she frowned. "I will take a careful look around for cameras and covert devices", I said, I have seen enough spy films to know what to look for. "Ok" she said with a cynical smile. I said "LUCIE", look, they have read all of our emails, texts, and chats without us even being aware, so I am erring on the side of caution. They are probably listening into us right now she said.

Testing 1, 2, 1, 2.

Well, it worked! We both got texts on our DIA mobiles both from Agent Green but each passing on information through specific channels. Lucie read hers out… *Hi Lucie this is AG forwarding info from your colleague Patrick and SETI who have also been collaborating since we connected them up. After your suggestion of using Intelligence buffers from the outer orbit satellites we believe we have enough directional information that points to an EXO planet we have called GL21persJGSW.*

I think you can work out the mnemonics.
Congratulations.

We are currently working out timings and distance
theories between the services, now driven by the DIA.
Keep this information to our group as always. AG

Lucie's lip quivered; "Stephen do you hear those
Mnemonics?" "Yes, but didn't quite get them like most
of those references, just a jumble of letters". "I think we
have our Swift Tuttle moment Stephen" she blurted.
"What!" "Well, GL21 is the Goldilocks year then
Perseids and then our initials, Lucie looked to be glazing
over with emotion.

My text from AG was actually from Agent Smith, Julia,
my sister. Stephen As you know we took your blood and
I also had my blood taken just after you left, and we had
them compared so we could identify before and after, so
to speak. Our Blood type is the same and our HLA
almost identical but for the anomalies we were looking
for.

I have shared this with David to see if he can come up
with any possible reasons as well as from our own
laboratories because we don't specialize quite as much
as you do.

A call out of the blue from David with agent green on
conference asked me to prepare for a customer service
call. What for I said. I got a call from Agent Green and
our own Rod from procurement he said, they are both
asking us to take a careful look into one of our biggest

customers over in Nevada. Not only have they requested tons of binding agent from us Stephen, but the DIA have discovered satellite photographs showing what looks like a chalk pit with faint lines near their small factory unit, but not on their doorstep. It does seem more than a little strange. It might be nothing at all but there isn't a quarry for two hundred miles that we know of, so we would like to know what it is. The huge order for a binding agent does not fit with such a small registered business of food production company nor does it match their previous orders. The company manufacture meat free alternatives called Clock Meet. Their motto is "About Time"

Stephen, they manufacture meat free burgers amongst other things and are about to sign a contract with an international fast-food chain. "I don't quite get it David" I said. "That seems quite normal, isn't it?"

Well, our agents may not be telling us the whole story.

"OK but I think they want us to confirm their suspicions, whatever they are! So that's for you and me to find out and a snoop at the factory may give us the proof they need". "Bio Science on the other hand are worried that their huge lucrative contract might be in jeopardy if we spoil it by rocking the boat, so softly does it. It might be that the new order is in anticipation of the contract being signed and completely innocent".

"I'll ask Lucie" I said "and see if she can get a connection with a LIDAR satellite that we can use for a scan at high definition". "David told us it had already been done which is how the CIA saw something unusual on the ground and passed it to the DIA and with a bit of research discovered that our work place BIOscience is a supplier for them".

"What was that Stephen", Lucie quipped, that I need to get a connection?

"Sorry Lucie but until David told me of his phone call with Julia, I didn't think you needed to be a part of the conversation that is until he mentioned a satellite scan.

I was going to ask you to connect with Patrick but the CIA and DIA have already commissioned a LIDAR scan and have the results they were looking for".

"Well, the fact that the DIA are involved makes me think it could be getting a little creepy and we might be well out of our depth".

"I take it this is secret Stephen, so we have to use channels that are under the radar. Do you want me to speak to Patrick and see what he can come up with?" "Perhaps I should ring agent Green first to see if their results are clear enough to work with". "Yes, not a bad idea" I said, "in case they have missed something".

"If you can find me the co-ordinates of the place you want me to have scanned, please Stephen, Longitude and latitude will be ok". "Alright I can get this from the company website" I said. "Is there a laptop in this house Lucie?" "How should I know" she said "ask big brother!"

No sooner said than pinged on both of our mobiles. *Laptop in kitchen unit under the microwave. The password will be texted to you as soon as you start the laptop. AG* OMG Lucie was not wrong.

"Shouldn't I speak to Agent Green though?"

"Well, the fact that you have a laptop from big brother and a reply without asking I think it is safe to say we have the go ahead".

Two buttons and texts later and we had the details and so did Patrick, assuming that he did have some access that met our needs. Patrick told us that he has new beta tested interpolation software that he knew worked but not issued yet that promised much finer lidar results, perhaps better than the suits currently had.

As soon as Lucie asked him, he said yes, I have clearance sent via your high-level connection almost God like speed. "You really do have friends in high places Lucie".

She gave the co-ordinates over and asked for a spread of about five miles all around from the obvious building that we were intending to visit.

Agent Green and Smith called us both on the mobile so we could conference together and suggested we get the laptop out again to video talk. They asked us to close the curtains and blinds and switch on the larder pantry light.

It apparently operated a spectrum jam with a notch for our own comms. We should use this whenever we are using any kind of communications was said btw.

Another text password and we were online with Lucie, myself and screens of Agent Green, Julia and a new Asian gentleman introduced as Raj. "Hi Lucie, Stephen, this is Raj our correspondent in India and Agent Smith of course". "Raj has an update from your trip Stephen with some alarming information. This is purely within our own secure circle guys. Raj, over to you".

"OK, hello everyone. We have spoken with two of the people left in the village with reference to your trip Stephen and Arun, they are now able to speak clearly with us and describe their human disaster.

They confirmed that lots of people were taken away by visitors that were not Indian nor recognisable as any particular race. These people appeared from nowhere and created an arch that was like a glowing tunnel entrance. Those left behind told us that they were unable to move when the two visitors pointed a kind of gun at them. They could see and hear everything but not move. Yet hundreds were moving and gathered in the square only to walk through the glowing tunnel.

A few people arrived in the square but like the two we managed to speak to; they were also frozen to the spot when the gun was directed at them. The only significant difference we could find is that those left behind were not faithful to their religion. Those that went into the tunnel have not come back yet.

We are hoping and praying for their safe return.

Shocked beyond belief, Lucie and I were saddened and exasperated at the whole episode.

"So, where have these people gone asked Lucie?"

"Your guess is as good as ours" Agent Green said "but the method of transportation is more in question".

"Well, I don't recall seeing any marks of any sort out of the ordinary" I said. No one was able to direct us to the actual point from where they were taken, let alone where or how exactly.

"Has anyone been back to investigate since Arun and I were there?" "Yes", said Agent Green "and no marks or debris could be seen in the vicinity pointed out by the only two people currently able to talk". I dare hardly utter words hinting at abduction or little green men but this does appear so weird as to conjure up absurd scenarios.

"Did you get any clues whatsoever" asked Lucie to everyone? The only fly in the ointment here was spotted by Stephen and Arun and that was the empty cans of corned beef and the few people left behind. That there was beef being eaten in a vegan and sacred land added to the cans discarded in the homes belonging to those left behind makes little sense. This is almost like being penalised for not following the cause.

"So how many were taken then" Lucie then asked. "About eight hundred and twenty" came the joint reply. "Oh my god this is beyond belief".

"That many missing and transported somewhere is just incredible. How do you transport that many people in one go?"

"Ok" Agent Green said, "thank you Raj and we will be in touch should anything arise, and if you will do the same, please, all the best". Raj dropped off the screen then.

"Lucie then uttered what we were all thinking, the logistics do not stack up with anything that we know, does it?" "No, you are right Lucie" said Julia, but not in a logical clear-cut manner as one would expect from a government agent.

"What about other numbers I asked remembering the screen at the command centre?" "Fivefold" said Agent Green "and rising". "Plus, the cases of Alpha gal and Pork cat-syndrome are still causing concern", he added.

Do you have any more details of our Goldilocks planet was Lucie's next question. Yes and no came the answer.

"We have seen the remnants of debris on the periphery of our detection coming from them but nothing that indicates anything to worry about".

"Oh", she said, "perhaps it's a bandwidth issue or even a speed beyond our understanding". "Sorry Lucie I don't get what you are alluding to". "Well, we can see in the visible spectrum obviously, but we are only able to detect in the ultra-violet and infra-red using equipment detectors. Then of course microwave and alpha beta gamma etc. Is it possible that there are other undetectable transmissions or dimensions?"

"Alright Lucie by definition if they are undetectable how do you suggest we detect them?"

"I am not one hundred percent sure but we analyse light, then download the full spectrum and chop the bandwidth down into chunks and expand that into detectable sections. A bit like looking at the Doppler shift amongst the frequencies". "Plus, amateur radio people transmit on single side band without a fundamental frequency. They start with one but supress the carrier.

To detect it you have to create the carrier again then you can detect the transmission".

Then Lucie went on to say, "if you refer to the many sightings of UAPs some in the shape of a silver yo-yo. I happen to know that they are so quick we only see them in a subliminal way registering in our brain. Well recordings of these have been made of these objects using cameras set at an extremely high frame rate allowing us to see them for more than one frame.

They clearly move at astonishing speeds as confirmed by the distance and frame rate".

"What defies explanation is their lack of noise considering they are travelling many times faster than the speed of sound.

It is a shame we didn't have high speed camera on The Perseids, that night".

"Right, I will pass this on to our people and perhaps talk to Cern in Switzerland and see if they can come up with a detection method. Thank you, Lucie".

I interjected, "Julia, this trip with my company and David or Rod, can you organise our transport to bring us together?"

"What exactly do you want me to do Stephen?" she said.

"Well, a rental car, or pick us both up as we are currently a couple of hundred miles away from each other as you know, and then we have to get to the processing company that you want us to take a look at".

"OK, we can take you both to a rendezvous point where there will be a bona-fide rental for you to drive as company reps". "Yes, that's what I am talking about, so it looks normal" I said. "Alright Stephen, big sis will do it for you" she said, dropping the serious tone for a second forgetting that we were on a conference call.

"We will pick you both up and take you to a place we have, that is secure, and can have a vehicle containing the equipment you will need". "What equipment?"

"Top Secret badges" I said sarcastically, Julia rolled her eyes, Lucie huffed "he does that"." Well what equipment could we possibly need for visiting reps from a food science company"?

"Evidence gathering," she said in a cross tone. "Ok please tell me more" I said "and I will try to be more like Bond than Clouseau".

"Right Stephen, this is a need-to-know basis and must not be divulged to any other person, do you understand?" Lucie was giving me daggers whilst Julia spoke so I knew I was on thin ice unless I behave.

"Yes of course". Lucie spoke about subliminal flashes and the only way to see them is via very fast film or refresh rate. "Well, thought out Lucie, but what you suggested already exists here at the agency. Not only that but we have a pair of glasses for you to wear Stephen" holding up what looked like a cool pair of sunglasses, "these will record very fast data from cleverly hidden cameras but, and this is very important, the recording can only last for twenty seconds due to memory space in the frames". "Can I be a part of this visit Julia", Lucie interrupted leaning forward, "especially given the method of this mission?"

Julia looked at me and Lucie through the screen and paused for a moment. "Lucie, do you think you could carry off a procurement officer role if questioned?"

"I think I would be pretty good to be honest. I have an analytical mind and a scientific one so as long as I have the information of their order that they have requested then I won't look stupid and will sound legit".

"OK" Julia said "but I will clear this with Rod and David which will make things a little easier, not having to get you both together when we have you Lucie here already".

"The company I am sure will be anxious not to have the company misrepresented here with Lucie pretending to be an employee. I think it would be pertinent Lucie if you go as a science officer for BIOscience, not too far removed from your title?" "Yes, that sounds quite good" Lucie replied. "OK Stephen with that?" as she looked directly at me. "Yes, that could work" I said. "Do you want to wear the glasses" I said to Lucie "and test your space timing theory?" She looked to the screen to see if Julia was going to allow this. Julia nodded. "That will work just as well, I think". "When you get to the edge of the LIDAR identified zone, we are hoping that what we see on the scan can also be seen on the ground. With that in mind there will be a small new vacuum car cleaner which must not be used for anything else except sucking up any debris or unusual dust where we send you. Now we expect that there may be cameras covering the area, even hidden ones if there are places to hide them. So, you will have to create a reason to stop that should look genuine". "Without being sexist," I said "could Lucie use the vacuum cleaner whilst I pretend to fix a flat tire?"

"What about Lucie being car sick and throwing up where you want to vacuum?". That would be even better Julia replied. Yes, "that sounds great" we said in unison.

"The vacuum can be used to pretend to clean up her sick?" "Can you have a mouthful of yoghurt Lucie, just before you have to get out of the car" I said, with a hint of a smirk?

If looks could kill that would be another one of my lives gone! "Yes, I suppose so", she said reluctantly.

"We may arrange for a state patrol to pull right behind you two giving you better cover for your mission so do not get worried when you see blues and twos flashing".

"Right" said Julia "I will contact Rod, David and BIOscience for official clearance. There may be a different story from BIOscience if they ring you Stephen so don't be alarmed if they sound weird". "Right, got it" I said.

"Are we going to arrange a visit with Clock Meet or just turn up without an appointment" I asked? "We think" said Julia "that out of the blue might be more beneficial as you never know when people are not prepared, they make mistakes".

 "OK I agree but they might turn us away and then we see nothing". "It's a risk we have to take Stephen".

"I will contact you via our phones once we have clearance and everything is setup" Julia said and signed off.

We said bye for now and looked at each other nervously.

Lucie said "this is quite scary Stephen, pretending to be someone else and telling lies whilst we act like detectives. I hope there will be instructions with the glasses. I doubt it I said because this is so secret, nothing can give the game away". "We can always speak to one of the agents via our phone" I added.

We sat watching television that evening and low and behold amongst medical adverts was a new one for Clock Meet a new meat free alternative that had fast food critics chomping at the bit. The tag line for the new addictive clock burger ¼ pounder was "It's about Time"

A play on words meaning it's about time you stopped eating animals. Playing right into the hands of vegetarian and vegan societies garnering more support for their incentive. They displayed a QR code on the screen which could be scanned for a free pack of eight fabulously addictive Clock burgers. Mail free.

Their logo was not a clock but a design taken from Sumerian or Egyptian hieroglyphs, meaning time.

nohoh (nhh)
"time"

Then more astounding was an advert following on and linked to Clock service dogs. Newly trained sniffer dogs with the ability to recognise real meat, especially in supposedly meat free products.

Vital for devout vegan and vegetarians?

 What is the world coming to, I ask myself. Then I realised that most food places do not allow dogs due to hygiene regulations so you would have to buy the product and let the dog sniff it then put it in the trash if the dog says no. "Who on earth would want such a thing?" I said to Lucie, raising an eyebrow at the same time. "NO, not funny" she said with crinkly eyes. I never replied to that one, just thought it was good joke.

"I think the world has caught on with the meat sickness syndrome as everyone is calling it. Using a dog for sniffing the meat that will not make you ill. This so-called clock meat is cashing in on the meat sickness bug".

"Are all these things linked Lucie said?" quizzically.

Well, I said "most of these viruses are zoonotic pathogens originating from contact or eating bush meat from bats, camels, birds, monkeys, gorillas, and who knows what the next one will be?".

"Ebola, Sars, Covid, Anthrax, HIV, Simian foamy virus all had their origins in contamination with animals and hygiene. Or were they created in a lab and genetically modified for germ warfare?" "Perhaps this is what Darwin meant by natural selection" I said with a smirk. Lucie gave me a strange look and said "remind me again of your profession". "Err, Biologist" I said with a smile. "So, you think Darwin was a believer in Karma, not survival of the fittest?" "Oh yes there is that" I said knowing full well it was winding her up. "You eat me I kill thousands of your kind is more of a Darwin award except it was education not stupidity".

"If we were all like you Lucie, we would be safe, I think".

"Although from my current research, the first signs of Ebola were from a couple of children in Africa bringing home a pair of dead fruit bats. We don't know if simply handling them was enough to contract the Ebola virus, but they did".

"Fifty years later bats have their habitat destroyed by us and so have changed their eating habits. Moving to apple orchards, they are messy eaters and drop half eaten fruit on the ground with spit containing the Nipah virus, a brain swelling virus from the same Flying Fox Bat".

"Originally their dropped apples were eaten by pigs which in turn were eaten by humans. Hey presto. Now pigs are not required to pass it on because we pick up apples without proper cleaning".

"Sorry Lucie that is the end of the lesson. Just wanted to add that leaving out meat might not be enough".

We were deciding what we would do the next day when we both received a text from The DIA and CIA and FBI making this scarier than the thought of real aliens.

The arrangements have been made; the cab will be with you at 8am and will deliver you to the car you are to use and will be typical of a sales rep vehicle for your company Stephen. The glasses will be in the trunk Lucie in a case with a combination code of your birthday. In addition to your first destination of the perimeter of clock meet we have arranged for a state trooper as mentioned before, to stop behind you to see why you have pulled over in a prohibited manner giving you better cover to take samples of the debris dust on the ground. He or she will write you out a ticket for stopping but it will not be legit, do not worry. Make sure you have your driver's licence Stephen.

Stop at the line that was identified by LIDAR and expect the trooper almost straight away. Keep the dialogue correct without gestures and movement that may give the game away. The DIA have more than a passing interest in this since new discoveries were made last week, so no pressure you two.

Remember Lucie the glasses have only twenty seconds of recording so make the most of it and be sure that you have a legitimate target. We suspect that you will know as soon as you see it. These types of operations are not usually run by locals so may lack tradition and language that will stick out a mile but they think they are quite normal.

The angle for you Stephen is that the large quantity requested by them from BIOscience. Corp. is more than the monthly output for all of your customers. Can this be in instalments?

Ask questions that they may not immediately know the answer to, this will catch them on the back foot so to speak. Something like with such a large quantity we may need to add a preservative to keep it for longer etc. will this be ok with your chemists?

If they have any brochures at reception, please bring one of everything back for analysis.

Stephen you are of course the Chemist not biologist in this instance and Lucie you are their science officer linked to Procurement that is why you are concerned about the quantity.

Bioscience need to stock more of the components to manufacture the binding agent, another excuse to use.

Any questions either by return text or via the video link on the laptop, remember the pantry / larder light if you do.

Good luck guys.

"Good God Lucie talk about being up to your neck in it" I said slightly exasperated by it all.

"What are you wearing Stephen, for the meeting I mean?"

"Smart but casual I thought. I have only ever been to one function where I had to look professional and that was for an expo". "Remember I am a Chemist" I said. "Yes", Lucie retorted "not a Chemistry teacher though". "So, do you think a suit without a tie?" "Yes, I suppose it would look smart without being too formal. No bow either". "No, I said the batteries are flat anyway". "Only you would have a spinning bow tie like a clown". "Just joking, I threw it out years ago. Well weeks to be exact".

"And you Lucie?" "Me what?" "What are you wearing?

Not that killer dress for sure?" "Is that the look I got then?" "Wow yeh I'll say, you looked a million dollars"

"Anything in black" I asked. "Trouser suit perhaps". "No but I do have a colourful suit but not a power dressing one". "I only brought a small selection of clothes Stephen, all good though". "Well from the ones I have seen so far, you would not be out of place at a fashion shoot". "I simply spend wisely and carefully Stephen" said the fashion Professor.

"Ok better go and check that our clothes are presentable".

"Do you have a badge or nameplate Stephen?" "No Lucie just my card but that won't be any good here as it says Biologist". "I wonder if our people can knock something up", she said nodding her head towards the ether and looking up?"

"I have no idea" I replied "but a text would be worth sending. I will do it".

So, I sent a text to Agent Green asking for business cards for us both.

Within a couple of minutes back came the reply, *in your rental. Read them first so you know how to introduce yourself. We have changed your profiles so they cannot google you and get the truth. Those profiles will revert back when this is over. We anticipated this a couple of days ago when we planned this.*

You will keep your first names but you are both Washingtons.

End of text.

As I read this out Lucie's eyeballs nearly popped out.

Then another text arrived. *Siblings.* Cheers Julia echoed in my head. Lucie's eyeballs retracted and became smiley.

"We must be twins then" I said "because we are the same age". Now the eyes were rolling.

"We better get some sleep" Julia said, "long day ahead little brother". "Ha-ha" from me.

Alarm set to 7am.

Then…

We need not have bothered because the lights came on at 6.45 and music playing for our wake-up call.

Clearly big brother **is** here.

We both had toast with preserve, soya spread, vegan style. Not had bacon and maple for weeks now. Must stop thinking about meat for the time being anyway.

8am on the dot the cab was outside. We looked each other up and down and nodded approval to ourselves just as siblings would do. We were driven for twenty minutes then in the middle of nowhere as before, stood a single car, miles from any signs of life. The cab partition opened to reveal a drawer with a set of keys. We left the security of the cab and opened the rental using the key, not the fob, that it seems, was disabled. A ploy to stop scanners no doubt.

A look in the trunk provided cards, sunglasses vacuum cleaner and a yoghurt for Lucie to throw up on cue.

I chose to drive, fitting in with our subterfuge.

The satnav automatically highlighted the destination but only with co-ordinates, no name. After over an hour the point of interest showed yoghurt time which was bizarre and funny. We know that the LIDAR point must be close by, so I slowed a little and pretended to drive with a slight wobble reminding Lucie what her next role would be.

The brakes were applied without me touching anything almost like the brake assist now fitted to some cars.

I saw the supposed line we were aiming for so I drove quite close to the edge of the road, the vehicle stopping automatically without any input from me. I got out to go around and open the passenger door to let my sick passenger out as the sound of a state trooper, lights flashing approached us. Ignoring the police, Lucie wobbled out, having already eaten a good mouthful of the yoghurt and threw up just as ordered. The State Trooper pulled up with all lights still flashing and a couple of whoops. I put my arm around Lucie as if to pacify her, knowing we may be observed from any angle. Lucie managed to aim her projectile vomit right on the barely visible line that we could see.

The troopers first words were "what you people doing out here in the middle of the wilderness". I started to talk then Lucie blurted out, "my brother is a shit driver officer; his driving is so bad he made me throw up". "Sorry to hear that ma'am" he said. Sir, to me, "can I see your driver's licence and insurance". "Sure, officer" I replied. "I am sorry sir but stopping here is a violation of state law so I am going to write you out a ticket, just long enough for you to clean up that mess pointing to the ground". "Yes, officer" I said getting out the new vacuum cleaner and sucking up the whitish dust avoiding the peach yoghurt. At least this sick smelt rather nice. Lucie looked at the trooper returning with the violation and pointed at me saying "argh brotherly love officer". "Yes, Ma'am I guess so".

"Where yawl heading," he asked? "Just a few miles away we said to a factory office". "Ok folks be on your way then. I used some tissues to pick up the "sick" and we moved on after putting the cleaner in the trunk and Lucie sporting the special glasses, albeit carefully.

There was only one discreet button on the side of the glasses with no other obvious blips bumps or switches.

We pulled into the parking lot of what looked like a small office with a temporary looking wooden constructed building at the rear, where we guessed housed the small processing plant. Not huge like the exceptionally larger order would have us believe.

The pristine rose-tinted glass office looked amazing and perhaps even better if we could gain entry.

The doors were locked at the sides and so was the semicircle entrance.

The ClockMeet logo on the front door also had a touch pad bell sign. Touching this appeared to do nothing but after a couple more tries it must have been working silently inside and possibly annoying someone in the office behind the partition. A very tall slim pale man came to the front door and opened it half way asking "what do you want?"

"We said we are following up from your request from Bioscience for a very large order of binding agent. May we come in to discuss it?" I said offering my card.

He turned to look at the back wall where a similar person stood and without saying a word or gesturing to them said in a very soft voice "yes that would be beautiful". Lucie and I momentarily glanced at each other, wishing we could laugh at his version of effeminate English.

We walked only a few yards to the counter to be greeted by three more lookalikes, like septuplets from the same mother who rose up behind the counter like a collection of silent movie organists.

It was very funny but we had to serious and stay cool.

One of the collectives asked "what is it you would like to know". Lucie spoke to them and as they turned to face her their eyes blinked independently. Immediately I saw Lucie hold the glasses for about three seconds. She asked "if there would be a problem supplying such a lot of binding agents in one load in terms of storage facilities". They all looked at each other at the same time making us want to laugh out loud like we were watching five ping pong ball clowns at Coney Island turning their heads together.

We managed to hold it in but might have displayed some reaction. Then Lucie added "what about a preservative to help storage like Potassium Sorbate or something similar?" Stoney silence like they were all accessing their telepathic database simultaneously, or just earpieces, it was very strange indeed.

Then out of the blue, a door opened, fortunately Lucie thought to press the button and keep it held, catching a glimpse of the rear of the office for another six or seven seconds. The person coming out of the door was a caricature all on their own. Like five stereotypes moulded into one. So, mesmerising we just stared for what seemed like ages in disbelief that someone could be this way. "Yes, that is OK" they said with a deep gruffly voice that did not match the rest of the persona. Again, this was so funny we both wanted to guffaw.

"So, no need for a preservative to be added then Lucie enquired?".

"No, we have one thank you, it is very nice".

"OK" we said together wishing to leave before we burst out laughing. "Thank you for seeing us" I said "at such short notice". Like five choirboys in unison, they said "bye" and all waved. "Well, blow me down with a feather" I said to Lucie that was simply hilarious.

She too was falling apart inside and wanted to howl with laughter.

We got in our rental and let loose as soon as we were out of sight of the office factory.

"It was so strange, like nothing I have ever witnessed" I said. "That was a ready written script for a brilliant comedy just from that scene alone".

"Amazing" Lucie said "I cannot remember seeing even one of the traits in any one person let alone such a collection".

"What do you think about their eyes?"

"Oh, stop for a second please, you just reminded me" she said "so I can return the glasses to their case". "Look out for the cop", I said "we shouldn't stop remember".

"That was weird too. What animal's eyes blinks independently?" "No idea I said". "What the glasses will reveal is going to be fascinating".

"Ok let's get back to our cab pickup. I am guessing we will be delivered to wherever they want to meet us".

I drove in the reverse direction to the one that we came in i.e. From the middle of nowhere.

The satnav showed 55 miles to go and soon enough we were directed to a space that filled with vans and cars.

We sat in the rental and seven men in black came towards us sending our heartbeats racing.

I recognised two of the agents and calmed down immediately. Three of the agents opened the trunk of our rental and took everything out including the glasses that Lucie used to record the strange behaviour of the "Meat

People". Agent Green came to talk to us with a slight grin as he walked over. We left our vehicle and stood together. "Well, done" he said, "the trooper reported that it went well and didn't think that we raised any obvious concerns". "How did you find the Clockmeet Company?" We looked at each other. "Weird" we both said. "Can't wait to look at the glasses recording to get an insight". "Believe me, you will find it so odd, it was hilarious. One of the people's eyes blinked independently of each other.

Lucie caught their blinking eyes on the glasses and had a glimpse into behind the scenes when one of the staff opened a door into the back office".

"When the car decided where we should stop, we were able to make out our target white line.

The whitish powder we vacuumed up was clear enough to see and amounts to about half a cup in the short time we had, easy collection without giving the game away".

"Can I have some of the powder I asked?" "No sorry Stephen if the contents are what we expect to see, it will be explosive and far too sensitive for the general population".

"We will get together in a couple of days and share what we can with you". "Jump in my vehicle and I will take you back to your safe house". "Who are the others here" I asked. "Well, erm, CIA, DIA, NSA, all showing an interest" he said. I don't know if it was meant as a joke or for real to be honest. If it was for real this was some scary situation, we have gotten mixed up in.

Agent Green said "we will be in touch in the next day or so, and as I have already said, arrange a meeting". "Do not share anything you saw today with any other person, email or text, do you understand?" Lucie and I looked at each other with a serious frown and silence. "Yes", we said in tandem. Agent Green did not take us home but to a waiting cab in a parking lot which did take us home.

We stayed silent in the cab not knowing if it was part of the MIB outfit. Even if it was, we still had to keep quiet.

We removed our badges that helped support the subterfuge at the meet factory just before we got out of the cab back at the house.

Once we got inside, we felt we could talk again, even though we were probably being listened to in the house.

"I know it was funny" Lucie said but I can't help think that we are in way over our heads". "Funny" I replied, "it was darn right hilarious". "I tried not to think too deep about what might be going on. I like the way all of those factory employees were kind of synchronised in their behaviour and the slight delay in answering questions as if they all had hidden earpieces just like our MIB agents". "They are not androids, are they?" "I have seen some very lifelike models that are really hard to tell apart".

"I tell you what only just occurred to me" I said "the smell in the meat company office and it was even stronger when they opened the door to the back, it reminded me of a trip I once took to a fishing port in Maine. You know when the tide is out and the seaweed left straddling the rocks leaves a briny tang aroma. Not horrible but not nice either, a bit like oysters".

"You won't get me eating anything that looks like it was blown out of a snotty infected nose". "Awe Lucie that was a disgusting description". "Sorry" she said "but I cannot stomach those slimy smelly things". "They are animals".

We made a drink and sat down together on the couch to watch some garbage on the TV as a bit of mental floss.

I said "just to clarify Lucie you are no longer my sister from this moment on" "Why did you need to state the obvious Stephen" "Just in case I wanted to kiss you Lucie without you shouting you are my brother. She turned to me to kiss me on the cheek but I got the timing just right and turned my head quickly to the right so she kissed my lips by accident.

I got away with it but it was also quite funny and helped remind us of the funny day we had but I lost that moment.

Yet more adverts selling meat free burgers followed by the strangest charity advert I have ever seen, asking for donations this time to support vegetarian sniffer dogs! Last time we saw them trying selling sniffer dogs for worried people. Whatever next. If the truth be known they could have used these to sniff out bogus horse meat in TV meal dinners scandal, if only we suspected it.

To me it was hilarious that someone deemed there was a market for a dog to sniff out food that might contain meat.

I immediately looked over to Lucie and grinned. "NO, I still don't want one thank you". Mind reader!!

"I wonder if it could detect a slug in your lettuce" I said jokingly. It was taken as a rhetorical question.

It had been a long day and a strange one too so we decided to call it a day and retire early. I made a drink for us to take to bed as a nightcap. I had a decaf coffee but Lucie opted for hot chocolate.

As I placed the drink down Lucie gave me another kiss holding my head so I could not turn to steal one on the lips but a chosen cheek.

Just after getting into bed, we both received texts which was good timing. Julia's message said that she would be with us at 8am on the dot.

True to form she was calling us to open the door at exactly 8 o'clock partly due to there being no door knocker or doorbell but there were several discrete cameras pointing in the direction of the street, roof, trees, backyard etc.

Top Secret

I wonder if the neighbours ever figured out that this did fit with the rest of the houses in the street. No noise, no cables on the building, no name on the mailbox, no clear windows to peep through.

Lucie opened the door to see Julia in civilian clothes with a rather large shopping bag.

Excited Lucie let her in expecting some wonderful clothes to try on but no.

Inside the entrance hall Julia fished out 2 black folders, one for each of us.

 Handing them over in turn we went over to our dining table and as directed opened them up.

Headed by a very official looking USA Central Intelligence Agency Pursuant to NSDD 84 Provision.

Non-disclosure agreement between

Mr Stephen Williams and the United States of America

My name address date of birth, social security number, passport number, blood type, eye colour and any distinguishing marks such as birth marks or tattoos. None for me. Not sure if Lucie had any, apart from those sweet dimples but perhaps tattoos? snigger!

I knew that this was pretty strict having top secret was the highest level of secrecy to adhere to.

Then there were consequences for breaking the secrecy code that read like an insurance document. Scanning down the wording was nearly as scary as some of the situations we have found ourselves in. Prison, loss of pension, loss of rights, possibly deportation to the salt mines of Siberia I don't doubt. No that could never happen not on Russian territory and us two full of useful info.

Julia asked if we had any questions regarding the agreement or its consequences.

"Ok I will witness this for Lucie but another agent will have to witness your agreement Stephen because I, being a family member cannot be your witness. I have a member of the agency waiting outside ready for you Stephen so let me know when you are ready to sign".

"Why is there a need to sign this at this late-stage" Lucie asked? "Well," Julia said "that the things you have seen and surmised, were almost circumstantial and easily denied as being true but we are entering into a much more serious phase. You will learn important information that is in the interest of national security. Some of what you have already seen and heard will not be common knowledge even to some of the General Chiefs of Staff".

"This access had to be agreed between the CIA, DIA, NSA and FBI. You are privileged to have such access you two.

You have earned the right to witness what we will show you later today but be warned it is not for the faint hearted".

I did skip through most of the pages believing that Lucie will be more thorough.

"Ok Julia I am ready to sign" I said. She used her earpiece to call the agent currently sat in a car a few houses away.

A tap at the door and in he came straight over to me and sat down to watch me sign, followed by his signature. Peter Moore A762, hmm, high calibre.

A simple nod to Julia and off he went. Julia gathered both documents and filed them back in her shopping bag then walked to the door. "We will be back at 2pm to take you to conference with other agents. Bye". A wink for me.

"Ok Lucie we have about four hours for a bite to eat where do you want to go?" "Pizza restaurant" she replied?

Yep, suits us both. Still can't have red meat and not sure about chicken but tuna or shrimp will be good. I really do hope they find a cure for Alpha Gal V2.

Lucie looked over and said "look on the bright side, I'm ok though". "Whatever girlfriend" I said, holding my hand up in the air. She never flinched!! Oh, my we are moving on. She didn't correct me or deny that she could be. Also, no longer her little brother, that was a relief.

I have micro planned in my head subtle moves to bring me and Lucie closer like turning the heating down on a few occasions in the hope that Lucie felt cold and shuffled closer to me on the sofa to keep warm. It sometimes worked, either that or she sets the heating higher without realising I had purposely turned it down.

Lucie is very clever so it might also be our little cat and mouse game that neither side wants to admit to playing.

So, we get our coats on ready to go out for a bite to eat but at the back of our minds wondering what the secret services have to scare us with next. I may be a pussy cat on swings and roundabouts but horror films do not scare me, in fact I can see through the effects and find them quite funny. I have been known to giggle rather than scream at sheer horror, much to the disgust of others around.

The local pizzeria was not too far to walk so we decided to do exactly that and save the cab fare. Shrimp and tuna was what I had planned to eat with plenty of chili. Lucie went for a straightforward Margarita also with chili but oil instead of flakes. She apparently gets flakes stuck in her teeth giving her a hot spot, spoiling the gentle hit.

We both ate our pizza like it was poison, gingerly nibbling a bit at a time feeling a bit sick during the thought processing of the reveal yet to come. It could be likened to eating a very cheesy pizza just before going on a rollercoaster knowing we might be seeing it again, on our lap, or on the head of the person in front.

We didn't manage to eat all of our pizza and abnormally opted to leave it rather than ask for a take-out box.

This was just as well because we didn't make it home, instead were bundled in a black van like a gentle kidnap. The agent already inside the vehicle apologised as soon as the door was closed. He also asked if we had been on the ghost train at Coney Island when we were little, what an odd question I thought.

"If we had experience of that, remember how shocked you were that first time, it might come in handy".

After about half an hour and feeling car sick, we drove underground into a car park somewhere. We couldn't see outside at all, it was just the echo that gave it away.

They opened the door to the van and helped us both out straight into a concrete bunker of sorts. I did not feel good after that ride in the dark. Lucie was fine and added to what I deemed to be ever so slightly smug.

I was never good on playground rides or fairground Waltzer or Tilt-a-Whirl, have I mentioned that?

Although this place was like a soulless collection of walls it felt warm like it was occupied all of the time.

The colours were plain, and nothing distinguished one wall or corridor from another making escape for Lucie and I difficult should there be a need.

Ω Omega

The few doors we passed had what looked like Greek letters on them. Some of the symbols meant nothing and were not in any language that I recognised.

We were led into a large room with more furnishings that we expected, making it feel, and look quite comfortable. There were a dozen chairs and bits of equipment on smaller tables with wires connecting them. I could see cameras in two of the corners and I guess a mirror on the longer wall was a two way for observation. I couldn't hear any sound at all, nothing. Presumably no screaming would be heard outside of this room either. I have no idea why I thought that the sound proof room was relevant as if we were going to be murdered in silence, heard by no one.

Anyway, we knew agent Green who met us as we left the van, just no sister Julia, aka agent Smith.

We sat down where we were directed to in the Omega named boardroom and at least five other people followed suit occupying most of the seats. Four of the new agents brought equipment with them including a laptop and the box I recognised as the one containing those special glasses that Lucie placed back in the trunk after our visit. It became apparent what they were about to show us, would shed light on the whole mystery, beyond our known beliefs.

I tried not to stare at the group currently sharing the room, suffice to say MIB was all the description required. They also shared curly earpieces so all of them may well be receiving instructions on how to conduct proceedings, I suppose.

One of the men spoke, "good afternoon, everyone I am Sigma". Ah so they were Greek letters I mumbled. Lucie gave me one of her looks, so the mumble must have been a bit too loud.

"Just to bring everyone up to speed we have the output from the Clockmeet visit and a few more agents who will share their findings.

Mu, can you update everyone here please". "Thank you, Sigma", he said with a hint of soft gentle Irish accent. The kind of accent that could send you to sleep reading a book; "before we reveal the edited and highlighted footage to everyone, we need to show our two intrepid scientists here a little more of the context to this situation. As I understand they have both signed NDA's so what we share here will stay here, is that understood Lucie and Stephen?"

A wobbly spoken "yes" from us both.

"Ok please open the laptop Agent Green and link the glasses".

"Lucie & Stephen as you know these glasses have an extremely fast frame rate of over 3000 frames per second and are currently coupled to the laptop via Bluetooth for live viewing, meaning the recording facility is disabled but they are scanning whatever they are looking at, as mentioned at a very fast frame rate. Agent Green, can you please put the glasses on".

"Lucie and Stephen please look at the laptop as we start the access programme". Immediately the programme started we saw the agent directly in front as a fine quality portrait of the agent. "Now scan around, Lucie, Stephen keep eyes fixed on the laptop". Woah! We both shrieked, me almost falling off the chair, stopped by Lucie and palpitations ten times worse than the ghost train I can tell you. The agent two down was NOT as we were seeing them but an animal of some sort. Like they were wearing a latex costume of a lizard / snake in bright green scaly skin. He or she held up two claw hands and we jumped again, it said "We are friends, we have been so for seventy years or more". Lucie was in tears, of joy or fright or wonder I do not know but we both had real difficulty taking in what we were seeing.

I have never known hyperventilation before because I have never witnessed it, but now I know what it is.

Shaking as we did; the saving grace was that we held on to the eaten pizza which at this moment stayed down.

"Now you are over the initial shock" agent Green said, there is more. Lucie and I held our breath and said "WHAT, isn't this enough, no offence to the creature" Lucie added. "None taken" it said. "I am called Carl here on Earth" he added. "May I", Carl said to Agent Green?

"Yes of course Carl". I looked over to Lucie whose makeup had started to run down her cheeks and her eyes were more Halloween than glamour.

He began… "We made first contact over seventy years ago with President Truman and agreed to keep our presence here on Earth secret, on the understanding that we could study our assisted human race but, in the process, cause no harm". Assisted? In my head.

"We have developed over centuries from beings not unlike yourselves. We were at your current technical stage several hundred thousand years ago. Our present form suits our planet but we have the capability of cloaking our look using persistence of vision as you call it. We could cloak permanently but the energy required would mean we could only manage short periods".

"I must stress to everyone here although most of you know we are not the same race as the creatures currently running Clockmeet". Creatures? Lucie and I looked at each other again. "Some may not recognise how different we are but our biological makeup is a mile away from our unwelcome new guests as are the senses we have, and the food sources we need to survive. We take what you might term supplements to reduce the side effects of breathing your atmosphere. These Clockmeet creatures will have difficulty adapting too, but they are saline water based and do need to frequently immerse themselves throughout the day".

Ah the sea water smell we detected, thought to self.

"We are more land based now having evolved away from water, hundreds of thousands of years ago. Both our species can communicate telepathically making life much quicker and easier. We cannot fully understand your unwelcome visitors telepathically but ironically, use some of your spoken languages on the rare occasions our paths have crossed. We are not related as a species even though there are similarities but we clashed thousands of years ago when they tried to invade our two local planets and one service moon. Fortunately for us we are more advanced in so many ways so we did not tolerate their presence in our region of space". "We refer to ourselves here as Squama, a version of your Lizard reptile family. We are not violent as a race but we reserve the right to defend ourselves. We are bound by convention in our local Parsec not to use weapons unless all avenues have been explored. We are also bound by the convention not to share our power technology to other primitive beings. Having witnessed many wars on your planet you will understand what I mean. We have stepped in a few times over the last thirty years disabling nuclear weapons where planet extinction may have been a result in our opinion. Unfortunately, the human race was kept in the dark when these foolish decisions were made and corrected by us". Lucie asked if they had any religion.

"You have no idea of the irony Lucie because many thousands of years before we made first contact, we visited your planet. Then our people were seen by many on your planet as Gods as depicted by the hundreds of carvings, that they etched on the stones we brought them. Then we wore helmets to protect us from your atmosphere, but successful genetic alterations allowed us to adapt to your atmosphere in time although we still take medication for some compensation".

"Now to a more pressing situation. The Clockmeet people are as you have witnessed are rather strange to the point as you put it, hilarious. Perhaps you may think the same of us.

Now Agent green please show the footage from Lucie's camera glasses recording".

A few movements of the mouse and we recognised the office of Clockmeet but the people we saw looked similar but noticeably different in some aspects compared to our new discovered friend Carl.

Then as Lucie caught the door opening my God, hundreds of them on some sort of production line as far as the glasses could see.

A much larger behind the façade of the office than the visible building that we entered.

"We needed to know what Clockmeet are actual doing here and the next investigation, provided by Stephen and Lucie assisted by Agent Trooper gathered vital evidence that may point to more than just creating meat free burgers. Agent Zeta, please take the rein".

"Thank you, Agent Green, well the white powder you gathered from a fake exit of the factory contains frighteningly morbid ingredients. I say fake exit because the registered premises you visited as you may have spotted is much smaller than the one that actually exists. That glimpse through the door gave an insight as to how big it really is. Their operation is huge so it stands to reason that every component part of the production will be scaled up, no pun intended Carl.

This is also why the white line is over half a mile from the official building perimeter.

We have friends over in the Uintah basin with equipment that can fly over here at night using deep penetrating radar linked with LIDAR, GPS at the same time to get the real operational size. Your friend Patrick, Lucie and his connections added to the whole picture. Also, and this is for Stephen, I thought I would mention that this is possibly why they are asking your company for tons of binding agent. It is simply due to the enormous size of their operation".

"Now the startling facts of the white powder you recovered. I used the description as morbid earlier because they are so unbelievable and shocking in equal measures. Although you asked for some of the sample Stephen which we denied you, your company investigator David, did receive a sample but from us anonymously therefore not linked to us to but they were still able to corroborate our own forensic DNA lab findings".

"I am sad to report that the white substance does contain calcium but not of carbonate but human bone complex calcium phosphate".

"Furthermore, hundreds of various DNA signatures were identified emanating from a massive culture spread from across the world. Further analysis is required in order to give more precise and accurate data to pinpoint the victim's origins. The automated process is very slow given the spread of victims. Fortunately, we have developed a process on bone powder called Promega bone DNA extraction as used in mass casualty situations around the world.

I am also so sorry to tell you Stephen that even worse, we have identified at least one area of the world familiar to you, specifically, India, where at least several of the DNA samples belong, this makes such grim reading, I am sorry to have to share these findings".

"With Carls help and guidance we rather stupidly stopped scanning for invaders many years ago for fear that we would be detected due to using technology that did not belong on Earth".

"The unintentional smoke screen that was created by multiple cranks and nutcases across the world which we also ignored rather foolishly.

"Operation Majestic, Grudge and Bluebook just to mention a few funded projects via shell companies, missed the warning signs too. The general press was far too busy delivering misinformation on everything that was reported. Had we examined every reported incident, we may have seen our old adversary creeping in behind the activity"

"Incidentally Roswell was not of Carls race or their earlier cousins but space tourists visiting for fun like you people visit the zoo. Their craft was not fit for the portal and crashed not long after entering Earths address".

Now it is my turn to shed a tear or two at this gigantic revelation of portals, Lucie still looking very shaken.

"We don't quite know how it got out but the wormhole portal that they use, is not unlike Stargate that you see as a work of fiction. Carl tells us that it was seen as a renegade soldier teasing us with exposure".

Carl then said "the big question is why do our earlier underdeveloped cousins come here to hunt humans? I think it has become clearer now we have all this information, but it is not going to make easy reading".

"The first time these early lizards visited was not long after we made contact although we had a reason to visit going back centuries. But they soon left when they recognised that we were already here. They established a small colony on Papua New Guinea and began eating humans although they left behind the habit that they created which unfortunately carried on as you may well know, for some years".

"Can you recognise them as cloaked" I asked? "Different cloak frequency but smell sets them apart" Carl replied.

"So why did you not know that they were here" I added feeling a little guilty posing this question. Agent Sigma interrupted, "Stephen, Carl is not here on trial but to help set the record straight mainly for you and Lucie given your involvement with data gathering" "I am sorry Carl, I didn't mean it as an accusation" Sigma then addressed the whole room suggesting they all leave with the exception of Agent Green, Lucie, Carl and myself. He added "everyone currently present here are very familiar with the role of Carl and his people. We have shared the most important facts gleaned so far, so we can all leave these four and allow them to better understand how we all fit together".

Lucie and I looked at each other for a millisecond knowing that we were about to be alone with a real alien.

Carl spoke once the boardroom emptied leaving just the four of us.

"Well, you two I understand you may have hundreds of questions that you would like to ask, most will have been asked before but perhaps I should give you a potted history of us, that may explain many of your potential queries".

"Your last question Stephen regarding how we could be so stupid not knowing a historic enemy was here under our nose without our knowledge" Now I felt like the accused. I got a look from Lucie, not the usual daggers but a toned-down poker face with a raised eyebrow.

"When we banished them from our local system, Carl continued, they had not established a base nor a home port so we didn't really understand or get to discover much of their lifestyle or their needs in terms of food or bodily functions or even reason for being on our very own planet".

"The debris we found under water after they left, gave some insight as to where they might establish a base or home if allowed to flourish".

"A tiny part of our planetary taught history does in fact study their race as a subject, but it is not a popular one with scholars or academics and not very comprehensive as mentioned".

"Stephen and Lucie, you I imagine have studied Charles and Erasmus Darwin for an insight into the evolution of Earth and the various stages it has endured over time".

"Stephen, I believe you may have set ideas about the human race but I can tell you that some of the missing links as you call them are partly to do with our interference". My lips are quivering as he spoke.

"27000 years ago, we recognised slow progress in your planetary evolution at this time and it was agreed that we should insert a component into your DNA that enabled speech".

My lips quivered so much I had to put my hand over my mouth with eyes streaming as Carl spoke. Everything I know is wrong. We are part of a massive experiment as conspiracy theorists have been saying for years. Lucie was just shaking her head in disbelief.

Carl, I said, "did your species seed the Earth?"

"No", he replied" "like many exoplanets it was bombarded by remnants of dissolved life forms from around the universe, some by comets, asteroids and entities like us exploding some of the aforementioned about to modify our own planet. We have known your planet for over 100,000 years and have watched it grow with interest".

"Unable to communicate with you for thousands of years we delivered quite a few cut stones from your quarries and engraved them with knowledge to help you understand the universe.

Most seem to have been ignored".

"We find it hilarious that you have made these places worth visiting as a tourist, with no clue what they mean. Using our gravitational shroud, it was easy to transport those massive stones and cut them with hand tools in the hope that you may look into the technology". "However, you never reached that far. We do have a lot of tourists that visit your planet for, really sorry Stephen, Amusement".

"When you master gravity and cloaking then travel will be far easier for everyone. We do influence your species and step in when you endanger your local solar system but technology must be left for you to discover".

"This Carl to us is so mind blowing and made worse that we are bound by our non-disclosures that we cannot speak of this or very little of what you have just told us".

Carl than posed a series of suggestions that we might use to promote investigations into our science without being labelled a loony or crank. I said "I feel sorry for those so-called loonies out there that dare to suggest some of the things that you are telling us are factual".

"Space travel eludes you at the moment" he said "but when you crack it, we will be there to guide you. Take note that acts of aggression towards celestial partners will be met with strict defence. Watching how you fight amongst yourselves does worry us somewhat".

 "We can disable your nuclear warheads and systems if we think you are on the road to self-destruct".

"When you find evidence of previous technology deep in the Earth you will realise that you have been here before". That statement alone is beyond scary.

My head is ready to explode. Lucie is just sat there, tears streaming down her face still, looking like the world is about to end again. "I can understand why our respective governments keep all of this from us Carl. We are finding this extremely difficult to absorb". Imagine what this would do to the general population of the civilised world let alone isolated tribes.

"Even as emotionally stable people we are disturbed by this Carl in the extreme. I cannot see a time when this can be common knowledge, it is so huge".

"These tourists Carl how do they travel here"?

"Our tourists use silver spherical drones through a portal Stephen. Being technology and not living matter they can port very easily. The sender can watch the drone live like a home video. These are used as a teaching aid on our planet. Watching your planet and others like you has helped us to survive". "You mean what not to do?" "Yes, something like that", he said.

"How do they travel so quickly" was my next question. "Well Stephen they have a gravitation drive creating a false space around them so they have no weight or mass, no friction so ions power them".

"In the electromagnetic spectrum, Lucy's eyes widened, we discovered a frequency that mimics reflection but not just the fundamental frequency but a modulated one creating a space that the sphere can inhabit so it has no defined shape, effectively, they are rarely seen when their cloaking device is initiated". Lucie remained open mouthed. "When you see petroleum on water the layer is so thin that the varying layers of the petrol are at the wavelength of each colour corresponding to their frequency. In there also is a reflective frequency. That, Carl said is perhaps more than I should have told you".

"I am unable to tell you the frequency but suffice to say Lucie it is definitely in the electromagnetic spectrum that you and the scientific community are familiar with. Furthermore Lucie, if the sphere is being attacked, we can produce harmonics from the fundamental and create false copies, albeit reduced in opacity. A bit like your butterflies Stephen with false eyes on their wings".

"Do our own military know this, Carl?" Lucie said. Agent Green chirped in, "sorry Lucie that is classified".

Carl said, "oh and blaming us for not detecting the lizard creatures on your planet, not ours".

Agent Green raised his eyebrows looking directly at me, "Lucie too".

"Firstly, Stephen we are not your baby minding service, Lucie smiled, and we are integrated into your society and have been for tens of years. Some like it here and stay, others don't and treat it as a holiday".

"Only a handful, your handful, not ours," I smirked, "are part of your military and so most of their time is spent on routine work. We do not have manned stations on all of our friends' planets; we simply assist where we can".

"These creatures," Carl continued, ironic or what I thought, "do have a collective pungent smell but only when there is a gathering of them. We do not have a strong sense of smell much like humans, so one or two Lizard types would not raise a sensory hit. Call them Iguanals if you like, due to the fact that they are a type of marine based Lizard".

"They clearly live under the sea being similar to marine Iguanas so out of sight for most of the time. They can travel much like us through portals with cloaking. Their telepathic mutterings will rarely be heard and again only if 2 or more are together. The fact that they have telepathy does not mean of the same language. Their beta waves may be the equivalent of one of ours with a few bottles of your beers. One oddity we have in our limited research is that they occasionally sneeze salt. A very useful tell-tale sign if they have been close by".

"We only became aware of their presence here when the DIA and FBI were alerted to a global increase in missing persons, and UAP sightings almost in the same month".

"Thank you, Carl," Agent Green said. "Lucie, Stephen are there any other questions you would like to ask Carl"?

"Yes, please" I said, "Carl can I ask what your diet consists of, thinking of how different you are from the Iguanal invaders".

"Yes, Stephen I suppose at the back of your mind with the recent findings from your and Lucie's trip you must wonder if we share creature habits".

"The answer is a resounding no. We are warm blooded much like yourselves and can tolerate a wide range of foods. We do supplement our Earth diet with holiday created packs from our planet that replace the nutrients that are hard to find here. We give birth in egg like cocoons similar to your Alligators. We lay in two lots selecting a hot area and a cool area thus having a mix of male and female species. We eat small insects like locusts and small mammals but move to larger animals when we reach 5 of your years. Before you ask yes, we would eat small lizards like the invaders but only juveniles. Their bodies if I remember right contain chemicals in high concentrations into adulthood that would be life threatening to us. Very similar to humans eating the liver of some sea creatures, like Polar bear and Walruses. We do not eat anything that talks. That's the moral high ground I thought to myself".

Changing the subject Lucie said "can you confirm that the origin of the invaders is from one of the Exoplanets we extrapolated from our satellite orbits?" Carl looked to Agent Green. Agent Green answered, "yes Lucie very close to that region".

Then Agent Green said Well we think this has been very informative for you all and quite enough for Carl who must be exhausted?

"I am fine" he said. Lucie added what about the dark side of the moon? Agent Green shook his head. Carl replied with a great retort saying it was a great album, to smirks from all attendees.

The door opened and Julia, Agent Smith came in to end the question-and-answer session and put an end to shocks for the moment, at least.

 She came to escort me and Lucie home, or so we thought.

"Something has been troubling me" Lucie muttered quietly. "What exactly "I said? "Well, you took nearly a day to get to India yet when you sent a text from the hotel just before you left for the police station you were back here albeit poorly in about three hours.

How did you manage that?" "I have no recollection" I replied and looked at the agents.

"Do you think Lucie that my sickness was purely down to food or transportation and gas sprays?" I looked at the agents in case they offered an explanation.

Carl and Agent Green shrugged their shoulders and said "perhaps the time difference was to blame".

Lucie replied with furrowed brows, and "really though".

Agent Smith, Julia, reminded both of us that we were bound by our ND agreements still. So, although we were told some amazing facts we were not at liberty to share or allude to them, to our scientific community.

Shrugging of shoulders was not a proper answer to Lucie's question.

Once we all begin to understand these properties, we may no longer regard them as alien technologies, unless of course, we hide the truth, as we do now from the population, and treat the enlightened as cranks and discredit their theories, simply because they believe the public could not handle the truth. Oh the irony.

"I only hope that the cloaking hints given by Carl were shared with the DIA, CIA, etc". Looking at Julia, she gave no clue. They must know? otherwise there was no point in telling us.

"The two aliens you are now familiar with and definitely do exist and have done so for many thousands of years. They look similar from your perspective, yet they are from different worlds... It is only through evolution convergence they appear to look similar", Carl said.

I asked Carl if he and his people had any powers other than telepathy expecting a million years of development may have paved the way to something extraordinary.

Carl gave me an exasperated look for a cloaked lizard, whatever that was, and said "Stephen, we are not Marvel or DC characters" and looked to Julia.

Julia gave me a look, then spoke with the intention of updating us with the current state of play re the Alpha-Gal2 research, ignoring the previous conversation.

Of great interest to me as my carnivorous tendencies were itching to launch into a big fat steak.

"We have made some progress" she said "in identifying the blood groups least susceptible to Alpha-Gal, that is B and AB. You can inject Adrenalin, Stephen or a strong antihistamine; however, this is the temporary cure for the original Alpha-Gal so not sure about the modified Version two".

"A blood test for LGE antibodies in your blood has been requested however we can only assume that is the same for reaction to the sugar, Galactose 1.3. on V1".

"The option to inject adrenalin a bit drastic not to mention zapping my heart just for a bit of meat", I replied, eyebrows again from Lucie and wrinkle eyes.

"The DIA science team have made the connection between the Clockmeet Iguana Lizards and the Perseid shower additional meteorites". "With help from Carl and his people they have confirmed that their home planet of the self-titled Clockmeet Lizards, The Iguanal, are definitely in the same region as the extrapolated directional source we saw that evening, using Lucie's guidance and suggestion".

"The ClockMeet are under 24hr surveillance and have been since your own meeting Stephen and Lucie. We are trying to establish their transport routes given that thousands of people have been taken, we believe by them, and processed somewhere in the world".

"We have discovered a chain of wealthy companies linked with the ClockMeet people some with transport infrastructure and others owning freezer storage.

Believe me we are examining every aspect of this stock market listed company and how it gained such wealth".

I saw Julia looking at agent Green in the boardroom and then looked directly at us two, eyes moving more than her head meaning take them out of here. She must have directed him to escort us just as it was getting interesting into a control room very similar to the one, we saw a few days ago, although it seems like weeks have passed. Julia then said "come with me and Mu, who joined us as we left. I will leave you in his capable hands and she left as we entered the new room. Was Mu an agent code, or his actual name?

This room door had the sign of a kind of triangle with a tail on the door label, so I assumed it to be Delta... No, it was Lambda.

Lucie pointed out that she used that symbol often as it refers to wavelength and often used for light calculations.

Inside the room we saw a very busy 3D map of the world in view and hundreds of flashing colour figures changing as we watched. Another suit we were not introduced to was already in the room and a couple more were sat at terminals. To the left was a windowed room with two people sat at terminals but looking into the main control room. Both had headsets and earpieces. At the back and on the right of the room was a door marked λ and ∞. CLEARANCE ONLY. Lucies eyes lit up when she saw this. "Light and Infinity? Buzz lightyear" I said? "Don't be stupid Stephen"

Here was the now familiar colour ring indicator. Orange was lit and static. I asked what the colour banded column was for. "Communications" came the reply from Mu. Ah that made sense, flashing then meant urgent.

Back In the Omega Boardroom.

"Ok everyone we will bring you all up to speed now our intrepid couple have moved to the Lambda control room. By the way there is no need to share any of this with them. This is a need-to-know basis only".

"Ongoing investigations into Clockmeet are now far and wide, way beyond our original findings.

This is reminiscent of a drugs network, spreading where money seems to be the driving force. The funding is extraordinary and only after sifting through shell companies like peeling the layers off a Matryoshka doll we now have a link with a very long established and reputable jewellery house. This will become clear later".

"The Clockmeet company connections even took us to Murmansk in Siberia and Sisimiut in Greenland. One of their subsidiaries currently have a licence to carry out scientific experiments the other side of the world in Antarctica under the permafrost. They describe their activities as core sampling and cataloguing without specifics. Is this a one off? we do not know. We will direct our satellite tracking and LIDAR to look deeper into their operation. A gruesome possibility is that it is a human freezer store".

"Satellite tracking and clandestine shipbuilding revealed two submarines not belonging to Russia but using their port docking facilities in Murmansk and Dudinka".

"The Russian Federation are not answering questions about this, so currently this is as much as we know.

Those submarines have been tracked to the Arctic but both lost close to Iceland in deep water".

"Sisimiut in Greenland is historically the largest port capable of servicing ships, but we have no satellite images of submarines visiting to date. So, the routes connecting the registered companies we are interested in add up to this undercover operation of epic proportions.

There may be more so we have to be vigilant. It is clear that these people are well established and may have infiltrated every part of our society, much like the drugs racket, this is going to be hard to crack, no pun intended".

"Incidentally the jewellery business is mainly gold based and only the high-end stuff. Ingots of various weights, chains, sovereigns, Dollars and 22ct gold rings. We have managed to buy a cheap ingot from them via one of our agents. in fact, we bought the lowest value we were allowed to buy under agency rules. Analysing the metal content down to non-destructive XRF testing does not match any of the registered gold foundries on the planet, that we know of".

"The company filed documents, will direct us to their gold supplier, but as this is an established and respectable company, we cannot risk destroying their reputation if everything checks out clear. A change of gold supplier may simply be on a price point, so close to the market value that no alarm bells have rung thus far".

"The fact that there is no match with any foundries only means it must be an underground illegal operation. The same ones used to melt duty free coins into ingots and then claim tax relief. However, in this case the X-Ray Fluorescence, XRF, does not match the metal impurities found in coins so it must be a different source. There is a tiny percentage of Iridium in the gold and also a tiny bit of Platinum so it could be recycled jewellery or as we may remember a layer of space dust crept into the mix, just like the KT boundary around the world as a result of course from the Chicxulub event. I see a couple of furrowed brows here in the room so for those dinosaurs with a short memory, you remember the asteroid that changed the world 66 million years ago smashing in to the Yucatan peninsula. Well, it's that one".

"Any chemists out there wondering if the Iridium has isotopes that set it apart, the short answer is no. There are 2 naturally occurring and both falling from space or pushed up due to volcanic activity".

Julia, Agent Green spoke. "I just had a horrible thought that some of the gold may be from the thousands of victims that have gone missing over the years, reminiscent of the Holocaust". "What a horrifying thought" she said. "Well, the gold analysis does not show silver but a lower percentage of Platinum so no teeth were in the mix but that does not rule out wedding rings sadly".

Julia, he continued, "the NSA, CIA and FBI are collectively looking into this multi-faceted company having had a flag raised by one of their subsidiaries for potential anti money laundering infractions. There is a danger of course of our own people being involved in this activity for a slice of the action and providing insider info and protection".

"Given the complicated structure unfolding here people I think we should gather all agencies involved and meet at the Theta control room where we can have sight of the story so far. What about the intrepid two Julia asked? Yes, agent Smith, but only after we have filtered the need-to-know data. Shall we say in four hours"? OK nods all around.

After what seemed like ages we were collected by Julia into yet another room symbol Theta.

As we entered, we saw everyone gathered led by Agent Green, it looked to be a similar layout to the first one we saw with a few extras.

However, Lucie and I looked at each other in puzzlement not quite understanding some of the depicted areas, pictograms and associated figures.

No colour bands were lit.

I looked very carefully at the display and recognised a code that we heard mention, A4f with A4d and A4c but were told then that it was classified. There were three of them on the chart that I could see.

Hex Code

It might be hexadecimal or simply a code to refer to or even an address equivalent in binary.

Lucie was staring into space, not literally, that was her day job but deep in thought then out of the blue said "you remember the Clockmeet people"? "We were so transfixed on their mannerisms we overlooked other clues that may be something or nothing, or is it?" "Well, spit it out" I said, "keeping me in suspense!" "Did their whole demeanour remind you of anyone?" "No, who?"

"It might sound silly but when I was little, I remember a really strange man on TV that spoke English like the Iguanas, he behaved in a similar soft effeminate manner and dressed like a chandelier adorned with gold".

"I think I know who you mean not that I was a young fan, but mom and dad used to find him fascinating. Do you mean Liberace?" "Yes". "So, your point is?" "Why do these people wear so much gold like costume jewellery?" "Was he one of them?" "He could have been". "Not being a follower of fashion, I said, in fact the fashion police follow me around; I have no idea".

"Perhaps they don't have to pay for it. It could be quite common on their planet and undervalued. Perhaps it reminds them of home". "Maybe it is status between their kind". "I know gold does not react with anything except acid mixes like Aqua Regia so under the sea will not affect it at all. Think of the lost gold coins in galleons spread around the world. They look brand new even after 500 years".

Agent Green listened intently to this seemingly meaningless nonsense and spoke quietly via his earpiece and lapel mic. I couldn't make out what he was saying but he obviously found something of interest in our conversation.

The recipient of his quiet word in our presence turned out to be Carl who confirmed to Agent Green that according to debris left behind under water after being expelled by them, they discovered gold in machinery from what looked like habitation pods and nurseries.

There was a sizeable gold residue left behind in pumps and crushed equipment which not only signified a lack of value to them but perhaps a plentiful supply of it.

It was Julia who let on what the conversation was about. Lucie asked if Carl's people had analysed the gold? Supposedly the same source as their extravagant jewellery.

"The Lizards didn't value Gold but perhaps wear it to fit in with the trashy characters they view on our TVs seemingly to fit in". "Ironically not realising at all that their demeanour and mannerisms made sure they stuck out like a sore thumb". At an early stage they realised how much gold is prized above all metals on this planet and used it to feed human greed for the unscrupulous and garner help and support for their hidden agenda. It's also ironic that the human helpers would themselves be affected by the indiscriminate shower of biological dosing across the planet and therefore Alpha-Gal2.

Like everyone on the planet eventually becoming potential food themselves.

Lucie and I were feeling a little frazzled by now and wanted a break from this constant assault on our brains.

We asked if we can call it a day and reconvene tomorrow if that was possible. Agent green replied "yes of course" after receiving a yes in his earpiece. "I will arrange transport to our mutual relief".

I am sure the look on our faces said it all. This is a normal day for security services but quite taxing for us both. Shortly our transport arrived and delivered both of us back to our safe house via the usual secure route.

Walking up to our place there was a stray flyer littering the floor promoting a new venue in town. I managed to read it without picking it off the floor. I thought no more of it until we simultaneously looked and sighed, needing something to clear our heads, a bit of mental floss so to speak. "We ought to do a Walmart trip" Lucie uttered "having only bare essentials left in the fridge and no luxuries at all". "I really fancy a Tiramisu or something similar". "When the going gets tough the tough go shopping eh Lucie". "Possibly but not for food, normally that refers to clothes Stephen". "Well for me it is food" I said. "Yes," she replied, "I can tell food is your priority over clothes she said eyeing a fashion victim, grinning like that proverbial cat again". "Then shall we go to that new café in town?" "It looks attractive" I said, "it's called Top Tier, supposedly hoping to attracting a more affluent clientele. Fancy a casual coffee then Lucie?"

"Yep, c'mon then, let's go shopping for the first time together and enjoy the break and go to Walmart, such fun I said, Lucie rolled her eyes and said in the words of the song" "if it makes you happy" We walked to the nearest metro and got off at the station only a short walk to the supermarket. It was quite a different experience for me being the first time ever shopping with a woman that wasn't Mom. I was able to pick stuff up without being told to put it back as well. We walked around the store and grabbed a few items without thinking about making a list. Back on the metro and one stop past our place and another short walk we spotted the new café bar and a small crowd smoking outside.

We were able to find a seat without a wait or guidance and a space next to us where we could hide our shopping sac.

A quick scan of the menu and a snack of peanut butter and banana on sourdough with a Colombian coffee was ordered by going to the bar counter. We were asked if we had any allergies or intolerances. I could hardly say yes red meat due to aliens. No was our answer.

Just what the doctor ordered. We were able to sit away from the crowd just so we could take in a life a million miles away from our current status.

Voyeurism can be so enlightening when viewing a different social class. Lots of wows and really over the top designer makes on display here. This was a show of wealth of epic proportions. Boob jobs and pouting lips lost the classy plot to excess though but amusing.

The atmosphere was buzzing with music and clinking of champagne flutes with bright quartz lights rotating slowly around the bar to add a glisten to the gems being flaunted.

Lucie was transfixed on a couple of men due to their body language, they were practically hiding in the corner, perhaps for privacy, who knows. Then she jumped and turned to me. "Hey, I have just seen a funny blink, you know like our new found non friends". "You mean sideways" I said? "Yes, I think so". "Now look around and note the lavish jewellery, some discrete and others not so". "Is there Wi-Fi here I wonder. I need to look for something".

"Why?" Lucie said. "Just hold on a moment. I scanned my mobile for any company selling high-speed camera glasses in the hope that there might be an industrial use for them like strobe tire fitting etc. I found one quite fast by normal standards but only 120fps which may not be enough to freeze any cloaking, so we will just have to hope for the best, buy one and try it". "Or you could have to have a spy handbag Lucie". "No, you will have to have a spy pen or bow tie, that doesn't spin and play silly music Stephen", "OK I get it".

"I will order the glasses and we will come back here in the hope those guys are regular visitors".

"Can you have it delivered to the Academy rather than the big brother abode Lucie suggested?" "I don't see why not," I said. "I am sure Professor Lintott won't mind, especially when we are allowed to tell him why".

I placed the order there and then with hope that a sooner purchase rather than later meant it may arrive earlier in the morning.

"Cmon lets go home and try and switch off, again!"

We walked home, no metro, with our earlier shopping in hand and still puzzled over the what ifs given that we may have a local alien of our own.

Is our old town a favourite place for aliens or is it just a lucky find? We might be surrounded by aliens or just the one? We looked at every person walking by that we saw expecting that we might see something odd about them, but no, nothing. We couldn't stare at everyone we passed, that would be weird.

We arrived home and decided to find something to take our minds off aliens. A small glass of best Californian Zinfandel each and we opted for Scrabble from the cabinet of games supplied in the house and became very competitive then started to argue over real names.

Just when we lost ourselves in the game, Lucie argued that the misspelt word she placed down on the board was the way aliens would spell it. Funny, but reminded us both what we were trying to forget, albeit temporarily. I allowed the word in the hope that I could create a silly word too and use the same excuse.

I had the letters to create BYGMIST which I knew was spelt wrong but rather than use the alien excuse I suggested it was an Italian fog. Lucie laughed almost straight away; lightning speed compared to the fair-trade coffee joke on our first night.

Lucie then finished her wine and sat next to me instead of opposite leaving the board game with its silly words.

She held my hand and asked, "are we going to be ok Stephen?" I looked directly into her eyes and said "I hope so Lucy, we are on the right side and have very powerful friends". She hugged me and kissed me with real sincerity and more feeling than any previous kiss.

We bid goodnight and sadly, went to our respective rooms.

We both woke about the same time, at around 8am, no doubt due to daylight creeping through the blinds.

I had a text as we were having breakfast informing me that my order will be delivered between 12.15 and 2.15.

"If it does arrive then we can go to the café Lucie as soon as I check that it out, is that a plan?" "Yes, ok" she said.

In the meantime, "Stephen, I am a touch concerned that these aliens that we are mingling with may have frighteningly advanced weapons way ahead of us underdeveloped humans, so rattling their cage might not be a good idea especially being out on a limb such as we are right now. Are you worried at all" she said not giving me a chance to answer her first statement. Not believing it to be rhetorical I said "not really thought it through". "I am more worried about the whole human race Lucie let alone little old us". "I know what you mean" she said and added that what we are witnessing could just be the tip of the iceberg.

"Shall we have a light bite here so we don't spend too long in the café I said thinking that we would have less time messing up and being spotted?"

"Good idea" Lucie said "I will see what we have just bought in our distracted shop". "Do you remember what we bought Stephen", looking at me? "No, not a clue I said only, no meat, I guess".

Lucie created a miniature platter of cheese, baby tomatoes, hummus, rice crackers and pickles.

Not my ideal snack but nice enough to keep hunger at bay. To be honest I think Lucie enjoys seeing me eat food in her lifestyle choice. She seems so happy when we eat together sharing exactly the same food.

To be honest I like watching her eat so lady like and working those cute dimples. Isn't biology wonderful, a split in the zygomaticus muscle and pretty dimples result. A splash of freckles would be nice.

We had eaten most of the food when I received a text saying that my parcel had been delivered. It was 12.30pm, great timing. I opted to fetch the packet leaving Lucie at home. I was faced with a cab or walk when Lucie blurted out "LOOK IN THE GARAGE". "Why?" "I had a nosey around yesterday and found a cycle there. I have no idea if it is electric or manual she added".

Just my luck, it was manual! With gears though. I haven't ridden a cycle since school, so here goes.

It was dry outside and quite warm so I opted for no coat. Starting was so difficult and the saddle extremely uncomfortable. I slipped the pedals twice and nearly fell off, hoping Lucie was not watching me make a fool of myself. Unlucky me, she was howling like a demented soul watching my every move through the blinds like a peeping tom.

Within a couple of minutes, I was out of sight and after a couple of blocks could see the academy in the distance, well the aerials and dishes on the roof anyway. When I arrived, I went to the admin reception and the secretary recognised me and held up my parcel. "I guess you have come for this?" "Yes, please" I replied and took possession of it and said "must get back to Lucie". The secretary raised her eyebrows and let out an ooh!

No idea what she thought was going on between us. Wishful thinking on my behalf no doubt.

The packet was in a plastic bag so I had to push it under my sweater in order to cycle back. It was only twenty minutes back so not too taxing but my butt was feeling worse for wear riding a rock-hard narrow seat even for that short period. Lucie was not looking out for me returning, the uncool damage was done.

Cycle away back in the garage and unpacking the glasses which looked quite normal. A quick read of the instructions, I know, not usual for a guy to read first then operate but I cannot afford to mess up. The glasses were not as sophisticated as the CIA ones having no memory on board but they were Bluetooth connected.

Lucie managed to set her mobile as a recorder from a pairing with the glasses. We tested them indoors to see if they worked. Looking at a table lamp in the house we could detect the 60Hz flickering so there was a chance they might work in the café.

Now we had to psyche ourselves up for the return visit to the café.

It was mid-afternoon so we gathered our composure ready to set off walking to Top Tier café. Lucy placed her arm around mine so as to appear a couple, I did not object and stole a cheeky kiss. I saw a wrinkle at the side of her eyes which for me was acceptance.

We had dressed quite smart knowing it was a classy place and wanted to merge with the clientele. We managed to choose where we wanted to sit with a good view of the majority of the customers. Lucie sat staring at her mobile just as so many young people do these days not scouring social media though or texting but setting my glasses to record on her phone. I could not see anything different wearing the glasses so I had to rely on Lucie for guidance. The only control on my glasses was a single button which toggled on or off. When I pressed the button a tiny lcd flashed at the top of the right lens with a grey R. Pressing again lost the R

We ordered two cappuccinos and sat close together, button pressed and her mobile carefully placed so only she could see the display. I casually scanned around slowly looking at every person in turn as if I was a nosey person. Lucie just sipped her drink quietly whilst keeping an eye on her screen. First scan nothing and for a good fifteen minutes not a flicker of anything. Then ow! A kick to my ankle as I was looking to a couple of men quite close by. Lucie squeezed my hand and kissed my cheek whispering "him in the sports jacket". I stayed focussed on the target then we both got a text on our secret mobiles. They read OUTSIDE NOW.

Oh, shit we are not alone. We finished our drink and left together. Outside we saw nothing so we started to walk home but only made a few yards when a van pulled up and we were swiftly pulled in.

139

We were met with unhappy agents Green and Smith. "What the hell do you think you are doing? This is not Columbo or Murder She Wrote you two". "This is serious stuff and you nearly blew it for us"." Not only were we there but our surveillance allowed us to see your cheap scanning glasses and so could anyone else including aliens at such a low frame rate. This has to stop now".

"We will take you back home and let our people deal with this situation. You alerted us to the café customers on your first visit but you should not have pursued it any further". "Perhaps with hindsight we could have informed you that we would be taking over and thank you for your discovery".

"We can however give you a project to undertake if you still want to be involved or allow you to bow out. Either way you are still bound by your ND agreements".

We both apologised for our maverick behaviour and agreed to see the multiagency tomorrow after we have a discussion between ourselves.

Agent Green and Julia took us home via the usual route.

Back inside the house we felt relieved that the situation was taken over and we were no longer a part of this discovery.

"Can I see the recording Lucie and see what you saw".

She took out her mobile and let me see the video.

It was not as clear cut as the CIA glasses at all but it was possible to see an occasional uncloaking.

It was more like a subliminal flicker.

There only appeared to be one alien blinking so perhaps they are integrating locally or even holidaying like Carl's people, or are they placed everywhere as informers or simply a dropout or a loner in our local area? We were only guessing, just like our secret services.

"I wonder if these cloaked Iguanas are allergic to any of our foods" I said to Lucie. "It would be useful to know if this one alien was able to eat anything on offer. If as is normally the case most people ordering food from establishments are asked if they have any dietary requirements to be aware of or any preferences".

"If the Top Tier café have C.C.T.V. recording it would be useful to hear their answers. The hope is that there is something that will hurt them chemically or biologically which can be used against them". "Yes Stephen", "did you get that agent?" looking up at the ceiling covert cameras.

"If they are only stealing vegans there must be something in meat eating bodies that harms them, could it be just a matter of a horrible taste". "What do you think Lucie?" "Well, this is on such a grand scale this must be necessity, not born out of a need for gourmet food Stephen".

"Well, I would like to think that there is something harmful in our human race that gives us some kind of protection from being eaten, not just a question of taste, God forbid". "Harmful please then, we can use this to eradicate these predators", she said. "This must be the whole purpose of giving everyone an allergy to meat, so we become food for the Iguanas.

The loaded meteor shower delivered the allergy inducing bug on a planetary scale inferring that their needs were enormous".

"Perhaps their planet is in trouble and their early foray of Earth gave them knowledge of a potential survival route for the future should the need arise".

"Carl may know why they were here in the first instance unless it was a scouting party, to "seek out new life and new civilisations". Am I watching too many Sc-fi shows?"

Will we ever know I ask myself. I suppose I, like many on the planet are now vulnerable but the most vulnerable must be the true vegans who have desirable bodies. Sadly, like those in India.

"Remember those television adverts for meat sniffing dogs Lucie quipped, they could be used to tag targets like me she said".

I just thought it was a unique selling point for devout vegans or sensitive people but realise that these dogs could be subverted for their own detection purposes.

Everything now seems to be taking a sinister turn.

 Out of the blue we had a text on our service mobiles again telling us to be outside at 8am to be picked up.

"Well, I wonder what that is all about, we have only been home a few hours after being reprimanded for going it alone, playing detective. "It must be important" I said, will agent green point at us both and say Lucie and Stephen, you're fired. "Stop being silly Stephen, something has clearly happened or they have had a meeting about us and going to cut us free". We left the house as requested and were swiftly pulled into a vehicle as before. Julia, agent Smith was our first recognisable contact. The vehicle took us into a familiar building and into one of the interview rooms in which we had already spent some time.

Julia stayed with us and 2 other agents joined us one of them was Carl our friendly alien.

The agent not familiar to us introduced himself as agent Severn. He said that "he was joint working with DIA and CIA investigating your recent liaison with a suspected alien at the Top Tier café". "We carried out our own operation there, almost jeopardised by you two I hasten to add and concluded that he was visiting there alone and indeed an alien". "The person he was in conversation was a local and simply shared a table and small talk". We have managed to detain him without involving any of the people present. After a short interview we now know that he had clocked you and Lucie and recognised your recording device. At this moment we do not know if he had shared this info with anyone else. "This means because of this you are currently classed as vulnerable people and must take every precaution possible in your daily life from now on. We will be assigning agents to monitor your whereabouts". Lucie and I looked at each other with apologetic eyes but the damage was done. In my head I thought *monitor our whereabouts?* You have done nothing but stalk us everywhere, omg.

Agent Severn added "your amateur glasses may have been rumbled but because they are so poor they may not be seen as a threat, more as a toy, if luck is on your side, that is".

Carl spoke up and reminded us of the superior intelligence of alien visitors so we should never underestimate their skills or technology. "As we intend keeping this alien in custody, we will have a chance to perform tests and telepathic interrogation albeit in a different language but our people can work out some of his thoughts. His jewellery has been locked away as we do with all remand prisoners which has given the department an opportunity to analyse his gold with XRF and compare its composition. I am not sure that you were party to the wider investigation recently when we found a link with our alien visitors and their business connections leading us to a whole host of companies from shipping to storage and jewellery.

 This is where we hope to make a connection. Their high-class jewellery trade is doing extremely well, surpassing all other traders of a similar nature, so something lucrative is happening".

Julia thanked Carl and turned around to welcome Marvin, Julia`s husband who had just entered the room. I recognised Marvin of course but he looks so smart and looks to be well known and respected from the familiar way they greet him.

"I am now able to tell you Stephen", Julia said, "that Marvin, is a very senior member of the secret services here she said with pride, because, he is an extremely intelligent stranded descendant of the early earth civilisation called the Sumerians". "Wow Julia just when I thought I could not be shocked anymore". "Me too" said Lucie, "truly amazing, it's an honour to meet you, Marvin".

"Over to you Marvin". "I arrived twenty years ago via a long-established worm hole which collapsed when an Earth destined corona mass ejection missed by a slim margin but scored a direct hit on the portal near the moons dark side, only hours after I had arrived on your planet. As a result of the high ionisation hit, the portal generator was splattered and it took five years to rebuild. My mission was to visit Earth as a high-level envoy to update the Sumerian high command on the progression of Earthlings, in every aspect. During the rebuild I met Julia who was my assigned staff member at the DIA with clearance for interplanetary communications". Julia took over. I stood dumbfounded.

"Marvin does share some DNA with humans having being part of the strain that joint seeded one part of the Earth hundreds of generations before him. Sadly, for me she said, his DNA underwent several mutations since the original seed thousands of years ago which meant his 23 chromosomes are not a biological match for any human, including me, even though you sometimes had your doubts Stephen, about me being human that is". "Only in jest" I said.

"Marvin has helped us to understand a great deal of our ancestry and even human evolution. He has an ability to read Cuneiform Stephen, similar to you learning Latin to help decipher old messages and stone engravings. I will leave Marvin to tell you himself at some time in the future. Some of his history is mind blowing by the way, not all of it is recorded or shared. He will tell you when he is ready. Be prepared for another revelation.

This mention of seeding is not a direct seed but a gene pool mixing in order to advance the tribes that they encountered".

Lucie then asked "where in the cosmos is your home planet Marvin?" Julia interrupted, "He can't tell you Lucie, for the security of his home planet" "Suffice to say that they are flourishing and in a very safe quadrant. When they contacted earth in the first instance, they established links so that Marvin could communicate and go home for a visit, if he wished. That took a while after portal destruction but communications side of things was much quicker".

My turn, I asked if "Carls's race and the Sumerians actually seeded earth at different times" "Yes" Marvin replied "but millions of years apart". "When Carls race

came here, humans were not established but were a tree dweller without the ability to use tools much like primates. However, we know that they had already survived more than one ice age in several pockets around the Earth, mainly in the equatorial regions at that time. "Our race "Carl said "is millions of years old and has evolved to meet our planetary needs over time". "We have the ability to modify our genetic makeup now that we fully understand it by switching genes off that have given us unwanted side effects and illnesses.
You humans also have a kind of Gene therapy but this is in the early stages of your medical research. Gene editing will be, how you will eradicate mutating cells by modifying immune cells to fight cancer.
In time you will achieve it just as we have.
We too had faulty genes and mutations that were mostly unwanted". "Thank you" I said, "the future looks promising if we survive this current situation".

The bands of yellow and violet lit up and started flashing. Ah so they must be Marvins colours?

Marvin held his hand to his ear to hear a message and excused himself and asked Carl to accompany him. As they walked out. Julia and Severn remained with Lucie & myself as they closed the door, Julia raised her eyebrows and part rolled her eyes.
"What has happened Julia" I said. "Not sure yet" she replied, "I was not copied in on the comms". "Do flashing lights mean urgent then?" "Yes" Julia answered.

Marvin returned and went over to speak to Julia as soon as he entered back into the room. Julia's face lit up as they talked.

She came over to Lucie and myself after speaking with him. "Well initially it is good news", she said. "Our Iguana prisoner has decided to tell all, or so it seems". "This may sound like a breakthrough but we have to be cautious, as this may not be as straight forward as it seems and the alien may be testing the water, no irony there".

"He has already been MRI scanned to see if he has any implants i.e. communication devices.

Correction *she* showed no implants and nothing except eggs, thanks to the MRI. We have given her the name Siren rather than her true name which is not pronounceable in our language".

"Our job it to make sure she is not able to talk to her kind, fortunately now her only communication route possible is via telepathy but that will need another of her kind close by.

Carl will have to guide us on how close they need to be to use that communication ability.

Siren's biological details were mapped and recorded and stored. She did ask for a saline water pond which we are about to arrange using a local diving school facility, in private as like us, they uncloak if going into water. Being a female of the species changes nothing except that we may provide a nest should we see any signs of that particular behaviour".

"Do they produce eggs without a mate", I asked. Julia had no idea, "again Carl may help us with this to a degree not forgetting that he is thousands or even millions of years apart from their origin". OK, yes, I remember evolutionary convergence. "Exactly".

"What about the gold jewellery we saw him, er, her wearing in the café Lucie interrupted, that is if she was still wearing it when you took her into custody.
Is it the same XRF signature that you have already recorded?" "I haven't been told Lucie but I will remind them to cross check. Currently her biological status is of great importance and may give us the lead we need to deal with them. Swabs and blood have been taken and food requirements including allergies and any unsavoury food no matter how weird. Could be a useful angle as you discussed Lucie regarding allergies or even poison".

"We will be growing cultures Stephen and producing a good stock for other labs to work with, including yours". "A full profile of Siren will be required but we cannot share this with people outside of our organisation which is why we want to find a weakness in their culture".

"When questioned why she wanted to help us, she informed us that she had been ostracised by her kind for wanting to integrate with humans even given the complexities involved. She also displayed guilt from their taking of humans to supply food to her kind. One instance that was mentioned dates back a few years when they tried to introduce a disease to stop humans eating meat. They had their own name for it but we called it mad cow disease. Not enough people stopped eating the tainted meat so that failed to give them the results they were looking for. She admitted that they had taken parts of cattle to experiment with but so many planet visitors decided to do the same in the hope that they would be first to find a way around the mammal meat issue for their kind. That created multiple mutilations around the planet which made humans investigate and we thought could blow our cover so our leaders forbade visits for this purpose alone".

Siren is not an important member of the invading Iguanas, so as a result she tells us that she only knows what is shared with their general population. They are in desperate need for food and sustenance. After many of our Earth years this planet is one of only a few in their search over millennia capable of meeting most of their needs. This planet is sadly the best match but for its atmosphere, but with biological manipulation it can be improved".

"We have given her assurances that she will come to no harm for her help. After all, if their planet is in trouble then there may be many more in her position".
"How is Carl with her, I asked, given their history?"
Julia said "it happened so long ago that many generations do not speak of it, only academics in a historical sense. Much like our world wars we have moved on". Marvin watched us like a table tennis match battle between wife and brother-in-law.
"You said there might be more of her kind wanting to join her in opposition to their struggle", I added?
Wouldn't that pose a much larger problem for you because they could converse without you knowing

exactly what they were saying, even plotting in a worst-case scenario?"

Julia replied "yes it could be difficult due to Carl only understanding bits of their telepathic mutterings.

Not to mention the physical needs of a group requiring saline dips periodically".

"What would you do if that happened" Julia? "Not my decision" she said and glanced over to Marvin. "I guess it might not be an answer we want to hear. Mind you how many humans have they killed Lucie butted in?" "I dare not ask" said Julia.

"The greatest dilemma here is for Carl and his people as to whether they intervene and use their technology to put an end to this. That of course would put earth in even more danger unable to defend itself against a superior entity without the help of Carls race. Not forgetting that they have a planetary rule not to engage their superior technology in inferior race conflicts.

We need a rapid response that stops them dead in their tracks, not literally but something that thwarts their efforts and measures with immediate effect".

"May I suggest something Marvin" I asked?

"Yes, go ahead Stephen". "Well as I understand it, these superior races have far advanced technology and could wipe others like us in a nano second so it is fortunate that we are friends, however is there anything in their constitution that forbids them to offer biological tweaking?"

In what way he said? Well, why don't we ask your people if they can help us with the inhibiting of the genomes that cause the mammalian Alpha-Gal syndrome? Should that be possible everyone on the planet could eat meat without the danger of anaphylactic shock and render their food source useless. Lucie abruptly joined in; cheers Stephen you propose to make eating meat a pre-requisite for life in order to survive! Not all I said, but if enough people around the world did add proper meat the percentage of non-meat eaters would not be worth the global effort.

"Ok" Lucie said "so we would be more of a delicacy?"

Marvins eyes crinkled at Lucies remark and thought for a second. You know Stephen you may have just had your Eureka moment. I will talk to our people and Carl to see if that "tinkering" as you put it is ethical for both of our races and feasible biologically. We as a race of human and hybrid integration know a thing or two about genetic engineering so we might be your best bet.

Wow I said, Julia did hint at your incredible history but never expected that, Marvin. We had teachers like you would never believe he said and technology that we did not have to invent, just learn.

A buzzer sounded and the coloured lighting bands were all flashing as if there was a fire or some kind of threat. Julia said right you two you must go, follow me and go home, we will contact you when this danger is over.

We were led through the now familiar corridors and out into the underground parking. There, one of the smaller black vans whisked us away and dropped us outside our house. No time for over the shoulder checking.

Back at the headquarters all hell had broken loose.

The gold that was sampled on the captive was of the same signature as the up-market gold the CIA purchased from the jewellery shop linked with Clockmeet, the fake meat people, plus the Antarctica research facility, Russian submarine docks and Greenland ports. Not unsurprisingly the gold attracted the attention of the Russian mafia who were acting as the go between for the meat storage in Antarctica and submarine manufacture in return for payment in cosmic gold. This gold was brought in by the aliens to buy greedy earthlings to do their dirty work. The gold was stored in huge amounts near the human meat storage underground in Antarctica, supposedly hidden from most humans.

The mafia hatched a plan to steal the gold and blow up the storage depot to cover their tracks. Ironically the value of gold was nothing to aliens but the tons of human meat was priceless.

There were no survivors and now no gold so the immense effort over months of processing, abduction and network of subterfuge was in tatters.

All of a sudden, Siren was shrieking and oozing salt from the corner of her eyes and holding her arms to her ear positions as in "the scream".

Carl was the first to ask her what was wrong, are you ill? No, no she said much, much worse. We are all in danger now. The commander has sent out our survival signal so we all told simultaneously through our telepathic receptors, leaving us all in no doubt what will happen next. I am really sorry, there is nothing I can do to stop this next level.

Siren said this is a powerful signal that can penetrate even rock and your concrete. I am afraid what your fellow humans have just done is seen as the highest level of aggression possible against us so the commander has elevated our position to plan B.

What is going to happen Carl said quite forceful and loud.

Siren spoke with more salt trickling from her eyes.

We are told to prepare to leave before the second sun rise or be left behind and be reset with the rest of the planet. This will happen seven of your days after we leave.

Carl asked what she meant by reset. I am not sure she said, but this happened when I was young and just old enough to understand. We heard of a planet that was going to be our new home but something happened and it was never spoken of again. Magical stories are read to us when we are young of a new planet being grown just for us but it will not be ready for five generations. The description is very much something you talk about all the time, another Genesis.

Where do you have to go then in the next two days asked Carl, so that you may join your people? I do not know yet she said but there will be a powerful signal again sent to all of our kind here on your planet.

Carl thanked Siren and asked for a meeting of the services through secure systems including the chiefs of staff that were not headless chickens.

Carl went to meet Marvin to try and establish what global weapons the Iguanas may have in their possession that is known about. Both of them made contact with their worlds to ascertain what if any info they have on this race and their past, given Siren spoke of a previous similar situation which may be recorded somewhere in the cosmos.

We were still at home wondering what had gone down that was so catastrophic that we were of no use.

I suppose given all the brains there and the ancient knowledge collectively it's amazing that we were able to offer any help whatsoever.

Well, the text came on our secret mobiles again to be ready, this time at 7am. Wow I said that's the middle of the night still. Lucie shaking her head, need your beauty sleep still? Just because you don't, I said, to a lovely smile.

Ok it must be early for a reason, we surmised.

Fake bacon and eggs far too early this morning. We were ready at 7am as instructed, not great after looking at my watch. It is telling me I did not have a very good sleep. According to the sleep app. Just ten minutes deep sleep and twenty minutes REM. Only two hours light sleep, not enough to deal with the trauma about to surface.

Bang on the dot 7am our ride is ready and waiting. No familiar faces when the door opened which was a bit disconcerting given the myriads of things happening. Ironically only a tiny part of the bad stuff. We hesitated for a moment then the MIB said c'mon Lucie you are keeping agent green waiting; time is important right now.

The van was blacked out and in a real hurry, not ideal for my anti-fairground constitution. I can confirm that it was not exhilarating like a fairground ride but a spinning in the dark playing havoc with my semicircular canals making me quite car sick. This time I kept quiet avoiding yet more ridicule.

When we arrived, we were led to an operations room that looked like all the others until we looked at the fine detail on the screens close up. Remember those codes Lucie at different points on that first screen that we saw, yes, she replied, well they now have another label in addition to their code but this one says Portal. Omg, they are not just for alien visitors then she nervously spluttered. No of course, not I said, because that is how Marvin arrived, if you remember? Ok but that was not on Earth, was it? No, ok it was the moon.

That was years ago, so they have discovered how to port on Earth then I suppose.

Julia was listening in to our gibberish with a wry smile. That would be funny if it wasn't for the current situation Lucie.

Which is? I asked. Are you ready for the shock of the century or it could be written if we get out of this, the shock of the planet? Go on we said almost together.

"Well, those blinking Iguanas have lost all their gold to greedy humans but in the process their huge stash of human bodies was destroyed by the perpetrators.

You may think great they will give up now and leave us alone but worse is to come". How could it possibly be worse Lucie said?

"Remember your blinking café customer Lucie now in our custody? Well, she was sent a global SOS signal that everyone of her people also received, telling them to prepare to vacate the Earth in several days once they agree on the assembly points. Presumably emergency portals or wormholes".

"That sounds good to me" Lucie said. "Yes, if that was all we had to be concerned about", Julia replied, "it might be considered to be best outcome, but that is not the worst of it".

"In their early years of education, they were told of a new home-world where everything will be ready to support their people in the near future".

"It would take the pressure off us" Lucie said. "Yes, indeed if it was ready now, but not only is it not ready, but it started out as a populated planet with human type beings living there", "just like ours" I interjected.

"They used a weapon to eradicate selected life forms and sow whatever they needed to, to sustain their population. We do not know the fine details".

"Oh, shit" Lucie said, "we are doomed".

"Exactly" Julia said. "This is as grave as it gets, she uttered". "Can we wreck their plan Julia, I said so they cannot escape and would have to cancel the world bomb?"

"Nice idea" she said" "but we have no idea what it is, or where it is. They may have portals hidden and craft waiting, or even outside help, we really don't know".

"We need to move to our central command and given the situation we have permission to take you with us".

We followed Julia through a door marked TS to what looked like an elevator foyer. The two doors facing us were AC and C. before I had a chance to ask Julia said clockwise and anticlockwise. Ok, Lucie said "a kind or circle metro?" "You could say that" she said. "We are going AC guys;" "ok" we said together. Julia nervously sniggered, "you will be ok Stephen, no need for a seasick pill". "Ok" I said.

Looking at Lucie she just raised her eyebrows a touch. The doors opened and there in front of us were several seats arranged, all facing left. The chamber was very smart being like a very large goods elevator.

When the doors opened, they were almost silent with no friction noise at all.

Sit anywhere she said and just keep still. "Are you sure I will be ok" I said to Julia? "Yes Stephen, grow a pair!" Lucie's turn to snigger. Julia said "go!" and we felt a little sideways movement and the seats all moved into a gentle angle as if counteracting a road camber.

There was no view only a countdown display of forty LED segments, all of the same red colour bar the two end ones that were green.

There was no need to worry as the movement felt was gentler than a skyscraper elevator.

The seats corrected and the door opened wide to a huge hall with masses of people and technology in sight that sent Lucie and me into a new reality.

I just could not believe my eyes.

We saw lizard type creatures and very small animals all clearly without any cloaking at all, some saying hello to Julia.

I asked Julia, those other rooms we have visited surely, they were the brains and control of everything you do?

No not at all Stephen they were just satellites of this, waving her hand in a half circle.

The Dome

This was like another world down here being so huge and even has the look and feel of outdoors. That's because she said that dome over there is a live view from another planet that we are currently exploring as an alternative home. I looked over to Lucie. She had streams of tears rolling down her cheeks and quivering lips as she took it all in. This time I suggested Lucie used a tissue to wipe her eyes to clear the bucket loads of tears and makeup debris that had accumulated in the last few hours without mentioning the horror movie look.

Not in my wildest dreams she said, tearfully, was this ever possible even for our children's future.

Encouraging I thought to myself. "Yes, our children may have a future" I said. She gave a lovely smile of comfort.

"What are the figures on the left" I asked of Julia. "They are the gases currently being measured on the surface in real time" she replied. "There is liquid water there and some oxygen in the atmosphere as you can see, but there are other undesirable gases also present. There were levels of methane and hydrogen sulphide showing in addition to ammonia". "Not a very hospitable place then, not to mention downright smelly" I said.

"The situation is improving" Julia said looking directly at me, "but very slowly things are progressing in the right direction Stephen, in an evolutionary type scenario".

"So, what are we doing here" I asked.

"We have been summoned to a meeting of all agents at this level of seniority and some visitors" Julia said.

"We will share the news however shocking and find a resolution, if at all possible".

This new Iguanal doom imposed upon us could be curtains for us all with no obvious way out.

"In a few minutes we are being asked to assemble in front of the domed screen.

I have not been briefed on what to expect".

Lucie and I scrutinised closely with wonder at the characters here with of course some of the black suits we have seen over the last week or so. Marvin and Carl were in the crowd talking to suits we didn't recognise but there were so many operatives here. "So, Julia do we have CIA, DIA, NSA and more in front of us?"

"Yes", she said "and a few more you will not know. Mufon, I asked? "Don't be silly" she said, "these are professional people here all in recognised departments not cranks". "AATIP then?" "Might be" she said. "No uniformed chiefs of staff visible here?" Julia grinned, "no we will let them know later otherwise they will be like headless chickens, flapping around and making stupid moves. Like going public or hinting to the press that we are on the edge of annihilation. That will cause mass panic amongst the population, shooting and looting and nothing to lose kind of attitude. I am afraid we have to keep our cards very close to our chest and take whatever comes".

"What *are* those small grey creatures Julia, without being rude and pointing at them?" "I can't tell you just yet" she said. "They all look the same" Lucie said "like the Osmonds or Korean military officers". "Apart from being three foot and grey with big eyes" I said with a grin. "I don't know how you can make light of such a situation" Lucie said in this dire mess. Julia said "he has always joked about everything, even when mom caught her coat in a car door and was dragged down the street, he made a joke of it".

Lucie gave me a scornful look which made me laugh even more. "It was funny though and mom didn't hurt herself, just wrecked her new white fluffy coat, it looked like a giant white rabbit had been run over by a Jeep".

"Stephen!" shouted Julia and Lucie together.

"I guess it is my way of dealing with it" I said. "Or not", Lucie quipped.

Over the Tannoy a voice said "please assemble in ten minutes from now in front of the screen".

My heart was pounding ten to the dozen then Lucie moved next to me and reached out to hold my hand. We shared a reassuring smile that said whatever happens we are together. The overall sound was completely unintelligible and collectively quite loud.

"Can you make any of it out" I asked Julia? "No nor will anyone else" she said "as some of these beings will be talking in their native language if you can call it that".

"Not through vocal cords in our sense but squeaks and bubbles and some via telepathy of sorts". "So how do they all communicate here then I asked"? "Note Stephen they all have earpieces, for those with recognisable ears anyway. We have a database of thousands of languages and dialects with seamless translation almost in real time".

"What about Marvin" I said "does he have some kind of device because he does seem to take his time to talk and reply?" "No" Julia said "he has learnt our language and spoke it fluently before he came to earth knowing he was meeting with a delegation here in America".

"So why", Julia interrupted before I could finish, "he is constantly weighing up every situation engages his brain before he speaks". "You should try it sometime" Lucie said looking at me. That tickled me and Julia so I had to concede that one.

"One minute to go" Julia said looking at us both. "Be ready for a shock whatever happens she said, I have an inkling of what we might witness here".

The strange gurgling of mixed languages and noises, the best way to describe them without laughing, was becoming quieter in anticipation of the address.

The screen complex started to display lines, big bang interference as it was called and lots of strange noises like a vocoder on helium. Then the screen cleared and a kind of voice tried to say hello but it was a choppy synthesized robotic kind of voice with what looked like a person wearing a horned hat, but not clear enough to make out much detail. The congregation responded with "hello" but in their own style or language. One synthesized moment later and the screen cleared to a weird looking "man" who was reminiscent of a Gandolf from Lord of the Rings only a lot taller although it was hard to tell without any other height reference. He was covered in Melam we learned later; a kind of coating that creates a wonderous look sometimes described as Ni.

A sort of glowing aurora coat of wonder, used for Kings and other Deities.

"I am Ruki" this rather tall person said.

"Who the hell is that!?" exclaimed Lucie quieter than one would expect given how scary it looked, hoping for an answer from Julia. "Our creator" she said through tears and a quivering lip shaking whilst speaking.

"What!" I almost shouted causing those in front of us to turn around.

"Just listen!" she said. The figure spoke again to say "Hello again" I am Ruki. "We were dismayed to hear that your kind are on the verge of extinction at the hands or should I say feet, of one of our failed experiments. For that we are asking for forgiveness and understanding that not everything we do in our historic past have produced good results. We need to thank our Sumerian friends Marvin, Carl and the accidental tourists for informing us of your predicament".

Furrowed brows from Lucie. Face as red as beetroot, Hmm.

"We watch you from afar, in actual fact many light years away and know that you, Planet Delta Ankh has created your own problems at times but you do not threaten other worlds, and this is why we feel we should intervene to correct our mistake in this instance".

"Sigma *7 was a poor choice for the Iguanal race as you call them, expecting them to flourish on a celestial body not fit for their needs, however this does not mean that they had the right to take another world from an established entity such as yourselves.

We have sent two Anunnaki envoys to the home planet of your enemy and to the planet that they have it seems already destroyed. Although you may not be happy about this but we have used our technology and power to accelerate their climate requirements one thousand of your years ahead of planned conditioning. We have removed every one of them including your captor from your planet so you are safe and will not suffer from these creatures again. They have been threatened with complete annihilation should they return or damage your planet any further".

"We will seed your planet (again) with a biological implant that will be fatal to the Iguanal but not to your species, including Lizards, Carl, and your native iguana".

None of us could speak for tears and adrenaline heads banging away like a Jack hammer, as we listened to this actual God.
All those years Lucie at Uni learning about our world and others and in actual fact we really know NOTHING. She was shaking her head and muttering *mind blowing*.

Then Carl and Marvin walked forward and bowed to the screen of the Anunnaki Leader as if he was a god. Well in Sumerian matters thousands of years ago they were THE Gods. Marvin thanked Ruki for saving our world and teaching us a valuable lesson. We will forever look up to you in so many ways Ruki.
The Anunnaki leader comically said "to use one of your comedy terms" "Live long and prosper".
Ruki stepped back from the camera or it zoomed back and we saw this massive Gandolf like man creature turn and walk.

The screen cleared and the planet set for our future was once more displayed through the multi-screen just then a massive noise emanated from the crowd that had gathered in front of us.

"What?" I said to Julia, "was that cheer about?" "Was it relief that it is all over?"

"Quite possibly" she said. "I turned to Lucie who was still red faced like a paper bag street drinker, sobbing uncontrollably like someone had poured the drink away. "Now what" I said to her? "LOOK" as she pointed to the gauges on the screen display.

They were edging up and down in the desired direction as we watched. I pointed to Lucie and shouted "Goldilocks!" "YES", she shouted back through a snotty nose. That could be our future!

Yes, without meat I added.

Look for the next book "Goldilocks"

About the Author

Timothy A. Smith almost became a bacteriologist with a giant food company in the north of England, but for a strange question from the interviewer about his Saturday job as a fifteen-year-old, really?

However, a downturn in the food industry shortly after, changed Tim's direction away from Chemistry, Biology and Physics, his qualified area, into Electronics.

Working on valve TV early on, later in colour, a new chapter and more complex engineering led to Jersey in the Channel Islands. Celebrities and millionaires abound. After six years in Jersey he landed a job in Surrey where asking for more money worked, the one and only time! That was for EMI and NASA producing data recorders that took everything shuttle Columbia could throw at it, for its crossing of the Earth.

Moving north again and with British Telecom Tim used some of his acquired skills later in R & D with their payphones.

Tim Married Andrea after joining BT then later teaching digital broadcast for 2 years and another move to the midlands to pursue a career in power electronics having gained an ONC in Electronics and an A* in Physics just for fun.

This new employer merged to become Rockwell, his final technical job, ironically the company who made the ill-fated tiles that allegedly fell off the shuttle during re-entry.

In amongst his collection of skills, add six archaeology digs, astronomy with several telescopes, firework making and electronics special effects for the theatres for 25 years.

Thank God he retired.

My thanks to The Sky at Night, BBC, for their inspiration going back forty years. Douglas Adams, Stephen Hawkins and more than a splash of Monty Python.

Mr Hoey Chemistry & Mr Grommet, both teachers.

Brian Cox

Carl Sagan above all.